Finding Hope

by

Bernadette Marie

5 Prince Publishing

This is a fictional work. The names, characters, incidents, places, and locations are solely the concepts and products of the author's imagination or are used to create a fictitious story and should not be construed as real.

5 PRINCE PUBLISHING AND BOOKS, LLC
PO Box 16507
Denver, CO 80216
www.5PrinceBooks.com

ISBN 13: 978-1-63112-020-6 ISBN 10: 1631120204
Finding Hope
Bernadette Marie
Copyright Bernadette Marie 2013
Published by 5 Prince Publishing

Credit: Front Cover Viola Estrella
Author Photo: Damon Kappel copyright 2009

Second Edition/Second Printing February 2014 Printed U.S.A.

5 PRINCE PUBLISHING AND BOOKS, LLC.

For Stan,
Thanks for finding me.

Acknowledgments

A very big thank you goes out to everyone who waited years for this book!

Thank you Fab 5 for all your love and support when I put my headphones on and go to work!

Thank you to my amazing husband for allowing me to create...always!

Thank you to my mom, dad, and sissy for always being right there to push the button the moment it comes out...if you're lucky!

Susan...oh, Susan! Here we are! She is here! Thank you. You have always been that silver lining and I'm so glad we get to travel on Cloud 9 together!

Connie...what can I say? You have helped keep my spirit high! Thank you!

Lesliann, thank you for giving me a once over!

To my readers...thanks for hanging in there!

Dear Reader,

Hope Kendal has taken quite a path to finally find her home here in *Finding Hope,* released (finally) by 5 Prince Publishing.

This lost third book in the Matchmaker Series has finally landed and I could not be happier.

It was great fun to watch Hope grow up from *Matchmakers* and *Encore.* And now she's finding love at the hands of matchmaking relatives—of course.

I hope you enjoy Hope's journey to find out who she really is and the small mysteries that entangle themselves in the pages of *Finding Hope.*

Happy Reading!
Bernadette Marie

Finding Hope

Chapter One

He'd seen it all in his chosen profession. The most popular: the cheating husband. There were bosses who suspected employees were skimming the till. And like the angry wives', the bosses' suspicions were usually correct. A missing relative or child was just as common, but this case piqued his interest more than most.

Trevor Jacobs looked down at the manila folder on the passenger seat of his car. He tugged at his collar. The Missouri summer was warming the inside of his car to temperatures that he was sure would kill a man. He picked up the folder and flipped it open.

Finding Mandy Marlow had been a challenge because she'd disappeared when she was seventeen. That had been forty years ago.

The last time her mother had seen her, Mandy'd had a newborn infant in her arms and had come back begging for money. Ruth Marlow, Mandy's mother, had given him the case's scant details over the phone. His notes clearly reflected that Mandy hadn't gone asking for a place to stay or for help with the baby. She had wanted ten thousand dollars and they had refused. She had told them she'd be living with friends. Friends who would love her and her baby, unlike her parents.

He'd finally tied Mandy to a David Kendal, a retired airline pilot living in Kansas City, Missouri.

Mandy Marlow had lived in the Kansas City area approximately seven years after she had left her parents' house. Her DMV records showed she'd lived in a house owned by David Kendal and exactly seventeen years after she'd last been seen by her family she changed her name to

Mandy Kendal. He'd searched marriage records, but he found no record that Mandy and David had actually been married. She had assumed the name through proper channels. However, their names did appear together on the birth certificates of Carissa Marlow Kendal and one Hope Katherine Kendal.

Hope Kendal had been born by cesarean moments after they had pronounced Mandy Kendal dead. She had died of heart failure and had papers that had strictly instructed that she not be revived.

She hadn't been.

David Kendal married a Sophia Burkhalter only three weeks later. He flipped through the notes. "In a lovely back yard ceremony of the home of the bride's grandmother Katherine Burkhalter," the newspaper clipping had stated. Adoption records showed that Sophia, now Kendal, had adopted Carissa, then seventeen, and the newborn Hope only three months after she'd been born.

What a tidy package, he thought. Ex-lover of the dead woman shares custody of his children with his new wife. What a twisted novel plot that would make. He laughed. However, armed with the facts he had, he knew it had been that simple.

A change of heart, or perhaps a shove in that direction, had Mandy Marlow—Mandy Kendal—giving up her children and refusing to fight for her own life.

Sweat beaded on his brow. Trevor reached for his bottle of water. It had grown warm. He drank it down and tossed it into the backseat with the other bottles he'd discarded there. He knew he wasn't the ideal patron for a car rental company.

He flipped through his notes again and stared into the face he'd become familiar with.

Hope Katherine Kendal.

She stood in a crowded room, but the camera had zoomed in on her. She'd been intrigued by something, or someone. Long blonde hair cascaded behind her shoulders and crystal blue eyes watched him from the photo. She had lips that were full and just a bit pouty. The face that mesmerized from the photo had a cherubic look to her, but a super model's features.

He knew he'd been fascinated by it too long, too many times. He'd seen it in his dreams. He'd found himself driving down the road thinking about her face.

Trevor checked his watch. He'd been sitting in the cemetery, in his parked car, for over two hours. He'd wait another two hours and then he'd move on.

But he didn't have to wait any longer.

A blue Miata pulled up between him and the headstone that read Mandy Marlow Kendal. The beautiful blonde that he'd familiarized himself with stood there in person. He felt his heart race a little faster.

The pace of his heart was different from when he was about to confront most of those whom he'd followed. That was adrenaline. This was lust.

Hope stood just outside her car. She was dressed in jeans that rode low on curvy hips. She wore her tie-dyed shirt tucked in, giving her a look of being taller than she was. Her hair fell well down her back in a long tail.

Large sunglasses shielded her eyes, but he knew how blue they were.

She wasn't moving. He was far enough from her he knew she couldn't see him, but he wondered what she was thinking when she stood still on the narrow dirt road. She reached through the open window of her car and pulled out a bouquet of flowers.

Another car pulled up behind her. Trevor watched with intrigue. Carissa Kendal Samuel—he'd familiarized himself with her face as well—climbed out of her car and approached Hope.

He watched them exchange a few words and then an embrace. It was amazing how different sisters could be. Hope was fair. Her blonde hair was strikingly different from the dark hair of her sister. Carissa stood a few inches taller than Hope and her figure was straighter where Hope's was voluptuous.

Arm in arm the sisters walked toward the grave of their birth mother. A smile crossed Trevor's lips. Right on time.

Carissa laced her arm through her sister's. "So, in twenty-three years this is the first time I caught you here?"

"You knew I came every year on the day that she died." On the anniversary of her own birth.

"I did." Carissa rested her head against her sister's. "I just wasn't sure why you did."

"She's a piece of me. She's a piece I don't know. A piece I'm afraid to ask about."

"We've always been open about her."

"I know. But I'm old enough to really understand. I think I want to understand now." Hope bent and laid the flowers on Mandy's grave then stood erect next to her sister again. "Do you really think she was always the person you knew?"

Carissa snorted out a laugh. "I hadn't thought about it. My memories of her aren't the happiest ones. I guess I never gave any consideration to who she was aside from that."

Hope gave her sister a nod. Since she'd been ten years old she'd been curious. She'd remembered asking her father on the day they had buried her great-grandmother, Katie, if he'd take her to see her birth mother's grave. She'd whispered it in his ear, not wanting to hurt her mother's feelings. He'd agreed. They hadn't gone that day, but he'd taken her.

They had stood where she now stood with her sister on her arm. They'd looked down at the grave without a word. She hadn't asked questions and he hadn't offered anything either. They just stood together in awkward silence.

The woman in the grave was not her mother. She understood that. Yes, Mandy had given birth to her, but that wasn't motherhood. Sophia was her mother and would remain in her heart as just that. She'd raised her, molded her, and above all else loved her unconditionally. However, Mandy Marlow Kendal's blood ran through her veins, and unlike her sister, whose biological father raised them both, Hope knew nothing of the two people who'd given her life.

Carissa gave her a nudge.

"I have to get back to the school. Thomas is planning dinner for you tonight. You are coming, aren't you?"

"Me miss a birthday dinner that Thomas made? Not on your life." She kissed her sister's cheek. "Tell him I'll be there and I'll bring treats for the kids."

"No candy," Carissa pleaded. "Aiden has had enough sweets since he's been staying with Mom while we work. Bryce's teeth are going to rot out from under his braces, and Julie and Becky, well they just don't need it."

"Okay. I get it. I won't let you know." Hope grinned up at her sister, who only shook her head.

"You're as bad as Mom."

"We're entitled."

"Wait till you have kids. You will curse her and her giving ways."

"I'll take your word for it."

They fell silent again.

"Are you going to stay?" Carissa asked.

"Yeah. I think I need a few more minutes."

"I'll see you tonight, then." Hope nodded without looking up. "Happy birthday," Carissa added.

Hope tilted her head up toward her sister and smiled. "Thanks."

Carissa walked back to her car, leaving her sister to gather her thoughts over the grave of Mandy Kendal.

He watched Carissa's car drive away. Finally, he thought. He couldn't take the heat inside the car any longer.

Trevor slipped his business card into his pocket, climbed from the car, and put on his sunglasses. He walked across the grounds, slowly, as though he were searching for a stone.

She looked up at him as he neared and gave him a smile. Not an affectionate one, but that of someone who knew if you were in a cemetery, someone there mattered to you.

He wiped a hand over his brow.

"Hot day."

"Sure is." Her voice rang in his ears, penetrating every part of him. He'd studied the face, memorized the eyes, but had never heard the angelic ring of her voice.

A smile slid over his lips. "Visiting? Is this your grandmother?" He nodded to the grave where she stood.

"My birth mother."

Trevor nodded again. She was specific, he thought.

Hope scanned a look over him, and though her eyes were still shielded by the sunglasses, a knot twisted in his stomach because she was looking right at him. Those eyes he'd studied in the picture and dreamed of at night focused on him.

"Are you searching for someone?"

"Yeah. My aunt is here somewhere." At least he wasn't lying. It was his great-great-aunt. Her grave marker read the year 1877, but he didn't need to give the details. "I always forget where she's buried."

Hope nodded. "Good luck finding her."

She turned to walk back toward her car.

This was the point in his findings, in a case like this, where he would introduce himself and tell her why he'd been sent to find her. He wasn't ready for that. He wasn't ready to hand her his card and say, "Your birth father is looking for you." He wasn't ready to put away the feeling he had when her eyes looked in his direction.

"I'm Trevor," he called out to her and she stopped. "Trevor Jacobs."

Hope turned back to him. "It's nice to meet you." She smiled warmly and continued back to her car.

"And you are?" He followed, then slowed, realizing he appeared too anxious.

"Are you following me?" She tilted down her sunglasses. The piercing blue eyes he knew so well looked right into him, and his heart slammed in his chest. He could barely breathe.

"I'm just new to the area. You know, trying to meet anyone I can." He looked around. "Anywhere I can." He laughed and she pushed up her glasses and studied him.

"Hope Kendal." She extended her hand to him.

He took it and the shock that zapped between them had them both pulling their hands away.

"Wow," he whispered as he looked down at his hand then back up to her.

"Shocking," she joked. "Well, Mr. Jacobs, it was nice to meet you. I hope you find your aunt."

He couldn't move.

Hope walked to her car and he watched as she drove away. He looked back at his hand. It still tingled.

"It was a sign, Hope Kendal." He turned back toward his car with a wide smile. "And I believe in signs."

He swung open the car door and crawled in behind the wheel.

Hope watched him climb into his car from her rearview mirror. He headed out of the cemetery in the opposite direction. When she was sure he was out of sight, she stopped the car with a jolt and took a deep breath.

She rubbed her hand on her pant leg, trying to ease the tingling in it. She shook her head. She could hear her great-grandmother telling her she would meet a man someday that would take her breath away. They were walking through a meadow, she recalled.

Hope moved her head from side to side, trying to ease the tension in her neck. She was losing her mind. She'd never walked in the meadow with her great-grandmother. She'd only been ten when Katie died and she'd been too frail to walk anywhere.

But it was her voice that Hope heard in her vivid dreams. It was clear.

Hope adjusted behind the wheel, checked her mirrors, and put the car back into drive. She wasn't going to worry about her sanity. She was fine. Everyone had dreams that meant a lot. She, however, had them often.

Katie Burkhalter had been in her dreams since she'd been a small girl. She understood that. That was remembering someone you loved. As she'd gotten older, Katie was only a memory. There were no more dreams.

When she turned twenty the dreams had returned.

She and Katie walked in meadows, painted pictures of flowers, and even played the piano together. That thought alone had her laugh. She'd taken piano lessons from the time she was eight. Her brother-in-law had had the patience of a saint as he tried to teach her, but she was no good. The daughter of a world-renowned cellist and the sister of one of the most sought-after music teachers in the area, Hope Kendal couldn't keep rhythm or play to save her soul. She'd started on the piano and moved on to other instruments. It was no use. She was not a musician.

She was an artist.

Hope didn't hear the world, she saw it in vivid color and texture. What her mother, sister, and brother-in-law could convey in music, she could convey on canvas.

Luck had been on her side. The small store next to her sister's music school had become available when she'd turned twenty-one. Already established as a mural artist, she opened a small gift shop where she could also sell her paintings and work on them as well. Business wasn't booming, but it kept her busy, happy, and close to her family.

Now, with her hand still tingling and her grandmother's voice ringing in her ears, she felt the need to paint. She drove back to her studio.

She would keep the store closed for the rest of the day. After all, it was her birthday. She deserved a day off, but she would paint. She would paint him.

Music filtered through the walls as Hope set up her canvas and selected a pencil to sketch the face of the stranger she'd met. Thomas had a student just beyond the wall that separated Hope's studio area from the music school. She recognized the muffled song. How many times had he tried to get her to play it? How many times had he not given up? How many times had she tried it? She was seventeen before they all decided her talents lay in another form. Painting was her avenue of expression.

Of course, her perseverance in playing the piano had stemmed from her being enamored with her brother-in-law.

She'd been eight when he'd walked into her life. Now he was the father of her two nieces and two nephews and still the light of her life. She knew how blessed she was to have two very stable and wonderful men in her life.

She began to block in the shading and planes of the face etched in her mind. The broad forehead accentuated by the short dark hair, the well-groomed brows that shadowed the deep-set, dark eyes, and the mouth… That mouth that housed a perfect set of white teeth behind perfect lips, which she was sure were soft, yet strong.

Hope lifted the pencil and looked down at the shadows on the white canvas. He stared up at her. She lifted her fingers to the canvas and felt the same shock travel through her fingers as she'd felt when he'd touched her.

Dear God, what was it about the man? Trevor Jacobs, she reminded herself, with his smile and his deep voice that still rang in her ears.

He'd happened upon her in a cemetery of all places. You didn't meet the man of your dreams in a cemetery.

She put down the pencil. The music from the school next door had stopped and she noticed that the light outside had dimmed. She'd been drawing the face of Trevor Jacobs for hours. She glanced down at her watch and decided she had just enough time to go home, shower, and change before she headed to her sister's house for dinner.

A smile slid across her lips. It was her birthday. Her twenty-third birthday to be exact, and she still loved blowing out candles and ripping into presents. Now it was even more fun. Her sister's children begged to help blow the candles, and little Becky, who had just turned six, was very fond of ripping paper off of gifts. It couldn't get any better than that.

Trevor watched the lights in the small apartment turn on as Hope walked from the door to the back, where he knew her bedroom must be. He hadn't actually gone through her apartment, but he'd studied her long enough. However, now that he'd spoken to her face-to-face he wasn't comfortable watching her. Before it had been to ensure that Hope Kendal was in fact the daughter of Mandy Marlow and his client, but now he sat in his car out in the street just because he wanted to be near her.

He tossed his head against the back of his seat. He'd never stopped from identifying himself when the time was right. His job had been to find a missing person. He'd done that. He'd found her buried in a cemetery in Kansas City, Missouri.

Once he'd found Mandy Marlow his job was to prove that she did indeed have a child that, by calculation, would be twenty-three years old. If in fact he found that there was a child, he was to contact his client and inform him of the findings. He'd done that. What a phone call that had been.

He'd told Donald Buchanan that he had found Mandy Marlow. The silence on the other end had been disturbing.

"How is she?" Donald had asked.

Trevor had frozen. Damn! The man hadn't known she was dead.

"Sir, she died twenty three years ago," he said cautiously and heard a sharp intake of breath on the other end of the line. There was more silence. "Sir, are you okay?"

"Yes. Yes." He cleared his throat. "I'm sorry. I guess I hoped that... well, it's not important."

"You were correct though. She did have a child that matches the age you gave me. In fact, she turned twenty-three today."

The silence on the other end of the line was different. He didn't hear deep breaths as he'd heard when he'd told him Mandy was dead. He was sure that if he could see Donald Buchanan, the man would be smiling.

"I knew it," he said simply. "You said she?"

"Yes, sir. A daughter." He was reluctant to give him her name. He still had half his fee to collect from the man, and he'd already finished what he'd been asked to do. Simply find Mandy Marlow and see if she had a child. He'd done that.

"Thank you."

"Just doing my job," he ensured him.

"I would like to meet with her, but my wife… she can't know about her."

"That will be up to you, sir. I can give her your contact information."

"No. She wouldn't know about me, would she?"

"Well she knew about Mandy, sir. She was at her grave today."

"Yes, but if Mandy died when she was so young, then she's been raised by another family, perhaps a family that has protected her from me all this time."

Trevor was sure of that.

Donald sighed into the phone.

"Can you spend more time there getting to know about them? I would like to know who they are and what they are like before I approach her."

"I'm not sure that's…"

"Please, Mr. Jacobs." He let out another sigh. "I've spent the past twenty-three years wishing I had found Mandy. I should never have let her disappear as I did. She was like that. She'd just disappear from your life. But I never forgot her." He was silent for a moment. "Mr. Jacobs, imagine being my age and just now finding you had a child. Wouldn't you want the best for that child?"

"Of course, sir."

"And wouldn't you want to ensure that child was comfortable in her life before you added any possible joy" he paused—"or misery to her life?"

Trevor closed his eyes and battled with himself. He could walk away. Investigating people's private lives was something of a hobby, a chance to earn extra money, and just a little dangerous sometimes too. It was living out a childhood fantasy. Going back to New York and investigating insurance frauds and claims paid the bills. His apartment was nice enough and so was his office. Things were comfortable.

But what if a woman did to him what Mandy Marlow had done to Donald Buchanan? What if he'd fathered a child and wasn't even given the knowledge that he was a father? What if his daughter had been given to her ex-lover to raise?

A sharp disgust began to brew in Trevor when he thought about the injustice that Mandy Marlow had done to Donald Buchanan. What if Hope wasn't happy in her life and Mandy had thrust her into a family that took her, but didn't love her?

Wouldn't it be his job to find out and offer Hope an alternative? What if she didn't like the Kendals at all? What if she'd always wished to be someone else? He could offer her something no one else could—the truth.

He'd have to accept Donald's offer, and of course, the fees that went along with that, and get to know Hope Kendal a little better before he could decide which path he should take in helping her.

"It shouldn't be a problem to get to know her better."

"Thank you for all that you're doing." Donald took a deep breath. "Mr. Jacobs, if I may ask, what is the first name of my daughter?"

Trevor contemplated what he was asking and realized that Donald hadn't asked for too much information. He too was keeping to the contract of what he'd asked Trevor to do. "Her name is Hope."

"Hope." Donald sighed. "Thank you."

The line went dead.

Trevor watched as the lights began to turn off in the apartment in the reverse order from how she'd turned them on. He also realized he'd stayed parked outside her apartment longer than he'd meant to. Donald Buchanan had asked him to find out about her family, he reminded himself. He ensured himself that was what he was doing. He'd follow her and see where she went. Maybe she'd lead him to her family.

He was just doing his job.

Then he saw her on her front stoop. She wore a short white dress. Her hair fell down her back in lazy curls. She locked the door to her apartment and hurried toward her car.

The thudding of his heart was a surprise. The sweating of his palms and the drying of his mouth combined into a clash of discomfort. He watched her now without the interest of a private investigator, but that of a protector. But whom was he protecting her from? He'd just moved into a very strange role of stalker, though the feelings inside of him were much different.

He needed to meet her again, and this time, get to know her—and stop following her like a voyeur. He drove away in the opposite direction, disgusted with himself for having sat on her street. He needed to justify himself again with a long hot shower and an ice-cold beer before he decided how he was going to approach Hope Kendal.

Hope climbed into her car as quickly as she could and locked the door. The tingling in her hand had returned when she'd locked the door to her apartment. She looked around. She could feel him.

She blew out a ragged breath as she started the car and turned onto the street. He was just in her mind, that was all. By tomorrow, she would have forgotten all about him.

She pulled up in front of the house where her great-grandmother and mother had grown up. Now her sister and her family lived in the house that almost a century earlier had been a boardinghouse.

Hope's nieces ran through the yard as she climbed out of her car.

"Auntie Hope!" Becky jumped into her arms. "You're going to let me help you open the book Mommy bought you, aren't you?"

"Becky!" Julie's eyes were wide as she stared in disbelief at her little sister. At eight she'd learned the fine art of keeping a secret. "Mom is going to kill you for telling her."

"I'm sure your mother won't kill her. But I won't tell her I know." Hope set Becky on the ground.

"Tell me you know what?"

Hope looked up to see her sister standing in the doorway with her arms crossed over her chest.

"That Becky told Auntie Hope what her present was," Julie told her mother, her voice filled with disgust.

Hope watched as a smile slid across her sister's lips and a laugh then escaped her throat.

Julie stomped her feet up the front steps to the house.

"Why are you laughing? Isn't she in trouble?"

Hope cocked an eyebrow at her sister. "I'm not getting a book, am I?"

Carissa stepped back so Hope and Becky could enter the house. "I knew someone would spill the beans. I guess you'll all be surprised, won't you?"

"Mom, that's not fair!" Becky protested.

"Well, I guess I knew you couldn't keep a secret," Carissa said as she patted her daughter on the bottom and sent her off laughing. "Mom, Dad, and Thomas are in the kitchen." She laced her arm with Hope's.

"You'll be glad to know I was working too hard to remember to buy treats."

"Glad to hear it. But you were working on your birthday?"

"Painting."

"Ah, you got inspired today?"

Hope stopped.

"I met a man today," she said and noticed that Carissa's eyes widened. "Right after you left, he walked by searching for his aunt's grave."

"Was he cute?"

Hope laughed. "Oh my God! He was amazing."

"You were painting him?"

"His face won't leave my mind. He shook my hand and there was such a shock that passed through us, I can still feel it." She clasped her hands together.

"And if I know you, you think that was a sign?" Carissa was studying her and Hope smiled at her sister.

"It was nice, that's all." She took her sister's arm again and they headed to the kitchen.

The aromas of Thomas's signature spaghetti sauce filled the house and had Hope's stomach growling. It was only then she realized she hadn't eaten anything since her bagel that morning before heading to the cemetery. Her mind had been too occupied to think of food.

Her father was the first to cross to her.

"Happy birthday, sweetheart." He kissed her on the cheek a smiled down at her.

David Kendal, father of the year, every year, in her book. She knew she'd only be happy when she found a man like her father.

He'd been a pilot up until the beginning of the year when he'd retired. Hope wasn't sure when he'd had time to work. He and her mother had been going nonstop since they'd cleaned up the retirement party.

They had traveled Europe and spent a month in Australia. They spent time in Italy with her former boss Pablo DiAngelo and his partner Pierre before returning home and planting the biggest garden in the city and taken on the role of babysitter for Carissa's children. Happiness was truly theirs.

He wore his sixty-three years handsomely. His hair was pure silver, but as he always said, "It let go of the color but at least it didn't let go."

Well-deserved lines peeked from the corners of his eyes. There had been a lot of world seen through them.

"Thank you, Daddy." She fell into his shoulder as he wrapped an arm around her.

"Stop hogging her." Sophia Kendal wiped her hands on a towel and crossed the kitchen to hug her. "Happy birthday, darling."

Her mother kissed her on the cheek and beamed at her. Hope couldn't imagine that a child born into a family could be more loved than she was. Luck had been on her side when her birth mother had given her to them. They hadn't chosen her, but they had taken her, and loved her.

"There's my girl!" Thomas put down his spoon and turned from the stove to envelop Hope in another hug. "I got your favorite almost finished. Why don't you get the kids to wash up and sit down?"

"I can do that much." Hope smiled at her brother-in-law. Carissa was a lucky woman. Sophia had set her sister and Thomas up to fall in love, just as her grandma Katie had done for Sophia and David years ago. Matchmaking. It seemed to be a family trait that lead to happiness. Hope could only assume they hadn't found the right man yet, or she'd have fallen willing victim to their skills as well.

As they gathered around the table Hope sat, as she often did, in awe of the commotion that ensued. Over the years, as each member of the family was added, she'd come accustomed to the changes at the table. Certain people sat in certain chairs. Some would eat their peas. Others would tuck them under other items on their plate to hide them.

Her sister never actually sat down, and her meal wasn't touched until her four beautiful children bounded from the table to find something better to do.

Thomas could carry on a conversation with every person at the table simultaneously. Her mother had taken on her great-grandmother's art of gossip. Never did Sophia say a harsh word though. She enjoyed sharing the happenings of those she knew.

Her father, as usual, was more reserved. He kept his words, she always mused, until he was ready to use them, and then he'd use them all.

Dinnertime at Carissa's was noisy, and messy, and always the one thing Hope looked forward to being a part of.

Thomas left the table and returned a moment later with a bottle of champagne. "I have something special for tonight. In honor of the birthday girl."

Hope smiled wide. "Oh, you shouldn't have."

"Can I have some?" Becky asked.

"You can have a little taste," Thomas promised, though Hope knew he wouldn't have his own. He didn't drink.

She'd never seen him drink. She'd been told that he drank plenty once. It had been enough to nearly kill him.

Thomas opened the bottle and sniffed it.

"I don't think you'll like it, Becky."

"Oh, it's an adult thing," she said with her face already scrunched up. Hope's heart went out to her. She'd been that girl not so long ago. With Carissa being seventeen years older than she was, she'd shared the table with adults her entire life and wanted to always be just like them.

Hope wrapped her arm around her niece's shoulders.

"Well, if you'd rather not have the bubbly stuff, then I think you should have a bigger piece of cake."

"Really, Auntie Hope? I can have a bigger piece of cake?"

"That is, if there is cake." She looked around at the others at the table.

Sophia crossed her arms over her chest and shot her chin up. "Have I ever missed baking you a birthday cake?"

"Not once." Hope reached across the table and placed her hand on her mother's.

Sophia Kendal, what an amazing woman. What woman took on the responsibility of another person's child and loved her like Sophia had loved her?

Hope sat back and sipped her champagne, listening to the chaos, and thinking. She'd battled with the thought for years. Had Mandy had a change of heart and given her to David because she actually loved her? Or was she hoping to punish him by dumping a baby on him and then dying? They'd all told her what he was willing to sacrifice to keep her, and she wasn't even his blood. He could have lost Sophia altogether, but he wanted to give Hope a home and he wanted her with her sister. Not a day had gone by in her life that she hadn't thanked God that David had decided to keep her and that Sophia had fallen in love with her.

Sophia carried the cake from the kitchen and set it in front of Hope. Precisely placed on the cake were twenty-three candles.

Becky snuggled in next to her aunt. "I counted them and put them on the cake."

"I think you put too many."

"Nope. Mama said to put two whole boxes on and then take one off."

"Well now that is one smart mama." Hope touched her head to her niece's as she watched Thomas light the candles on her cake.

This family, her real family, was all the family she would ever need.

Chapter Two

He'd paced the floor of his hotel room all night. Can you spend more time there getting to know about them? I would like to know who they are and what they are like before I approach her. Donald Buchanan's words had rung in his ears.

Now standing outside of the Kendal/Samuel School of Music, he heard them again and verified to himself that he was standing there at Donald Buchanan's request. He'd watched Thomas Samuel, co-owner of the school and brother-in-law to Hope, unlock the door an hour earlier. The first set of students had walked in. He'd counted eight of them. They walked back out forty-five minutes later. Not one had an instrument; they carried only notebooks.

Trevor left the comforts of his rental car and walked across the street to the school. He stopped briefly outside Hope's shop. It was still dark. According to the sign on the door, it would be open in the next hour. He gazed into the window past the collectibles neatly arranged on the shelves. The artwork covering the walls commanded his attention, specifically a picture of a hummingbird, which he was sure his mother had a small print of in her office.

"Well, Ms. Kendal, you certainly are talented," he muttered to himself.

He knew he'd be entering the store within that next hour. He wondered if Hope would open it or if she had employees. He'd never seen anyone else close up the store, but he wondered. Again, he felt the tingle in his palm and he rubbed it against the leg of his pants. Was he ready to see her again?

The bell above the door rang as Trevor entered the school. The room was welcoming. A coffeepot sat full, freshly brewed, and magazines lay out. A waiting room for the parents of students, he assumed.

"Hello. How can I help you?" Thomas appeared from the back.

"Hi. Well." He gave some thought as to what he was doing there. Every time he'd faced someone for information it was like a game. This time it felt dirty. "I'm looking for information on your school. I have a niece looking for music lessons and I told my sister I'd see what was available." Not a lie, though his sister lived in New York and would probably be able to find a closer school.

"Wonderful. I'm Thomas Samuel," he said, shaking Trevor's hand. "My wife and I own the school. Let me show you around."

Trevor followed Thomas back down a hallway.

"This is our piano room. I teach the piano lessons. Across the hall, we have two more rooms where we teach all instruments. My wife is a cellist and so is her mother." He waited for Trevor's nod acknowledging the "news" before moving on. "This is our theory study room. Before any lessons start, we have a week study course on theory. Then as the student advances, we hold advanced theory classes. My last class just finished."

That would be why none of the students had instruments when they'd entered and left the school.

"Back here we hold bigger classes," he said as Trevor walked through the door of the biggest room so far. "We have quite a few homeschooled students. They have their own band and their own orchestra as well. This is where we practice with them."

"Does the store next door mind all the noise?"

Thomas laughed. "No. Hope grew up around the students and was one herself once. She's my sister-in-law," he added with congenial love in his eyes. "She was my very first student, but her talents lie in art, not in music."

"She doesn't play?"

"Oh, she can, but let's just say she's a better artist." Thomas laughed again as he walked back through the school. "What does your niece play?"

Trevor followed him to the waiting room, racking his brain. "I think the piano. I'm just doing some footwork for her. They live in New York now." He left it at that and knew Thomas would assume they'd be moving to Kansas City.

"Let me get you a pamphlet on the school and you can send it to her. When are they moving to the area?"

"I don't know the time frame," he said as he cleared his throat, knowing it was never. "But I know if I can give her some information, that'll help Sarah settle into a new place."

"Your niece is Sarah?" Thomas's eyes widened, and a smile pushed at his cheeks.

Trevor nodded.

"I had a sister named Sarah." Thomas's voice softened. "Well, I look forward to meeting your family. I'm sorry, I don't think I got your name."

"Trevor. Trevor Jacobs." As they shook hands again, he heard the distant slam of a door.

Thomas smiled. "Sounds like Hope is at work. She'll have the store open early today. That was the sound of my arms are too full and I've kicked shut the door."

It was obvious the man knew her well.

Trevor would have known she was close even without Thomas's confirmation. She was within a few feet of him and his entire body had begun to tingle. "Mr. Samuel, thank you for the tour and the information."

"My pleasure, have a nice day."

She was making her second trip to the car. Why did she think it was so important to have fresh coffee and flowers displayed for her guests? Guests, she laughed to herself. Most stores called them customers. Hope thought of those who took the time to enter her shop as guests.

She tucked the fresh flowers into the crook of her arm, balanced the brown paper bag of plastic cups and individual sugar packets in the other arm. With her fingers tangled around her keys, she hit the button on her key fob and set the alarm. She turned back toward the shop when the door to the school opened up.

From the corner of her eye she saw a man, but it was the feeling that flooded her that made her think of the man that had encompassed her every thought for the past day. As she reached the door, the hand that came in front of her reaching for the handle wasn't hers. She looked up and froze.

Words stuck in her throat and the mere thank-you that should have flowed out was strangling her.

"Let me get that for you." His voice rang in her ears as he pushed open the door to the store and she stumbled through it. He reached quickly and grabbed the bag from her arms. His fingers brushed hers, and again there was that electricity that she'd felt the day before.

He was laughing. Words wouldn't come to her mind, but she could seriously wonder if something had smeared across her face.

"I guess we have something electric between us, don't we?" He was joking with her.

All Hope could do was nod. Trevor. His name came to her and she took a breath. "Trevor, right?"

"Yes, and you were Hope?"

She nodded and then forced herself to close her mouth. He was there. Fate had stepped in and brought him to her. In her dreams her great-grandma Katie had said a man would come and take her breath away. The words repeated in her head. He was standing before her, in her shop, and her breath had been taken away. Now, she thought, he was a guest. She needed to offer him something. "Can I get you something to drink?"

"Maybe after you tell me where would you like me to put this?" he asked, hefting the bag held in his hands.

"Oh. Sorry. Follow me."

She started toward the back of the store. The room wasn't big, but it was big enough for her to paint her creations and make a pot of coffee.

"So this is where you work? I was admiring your paintings from the window this morning."

"Yeah," was all she could manage.

"You're very talented."

"Thank you."

"I was most taken by the sunset near the front. Did you paint that?"

"Yes." She began busying herself with unpacking the bags and putting the flowers in a vase. "It was my first painting we made prints of. I sold a few copies."

"And one of them hangs in my mother's office."

"Really?" Her head came up and met his eyes, and once again her breath was sucked from her lungs. "Were you visiting the music school?"

"Getting information for my niece."

"I highly recommend it."

"I'll bet." He laughed. "Your brother-in-law said you were his first student."

Trevor's laugh fluttered in her chest, and she laughed too at the thought then went back to arranging the flowers. "Well if you can call me that. Trust me, I'm a better artist."

"So I see." His voice had changed and she turned to see why.

He was staring at the drawing she'd made of him after she'd returned to the store. There was no doubt he recognized it.

The pounding her heart had been doing since she'd seen the stranger in the cemetery was nothing compared to the pounding she felt at that moment.

"I'm so sorry." She wanted to take the canvas and slice right through it, but her feet were planted to the ground.

"Sorry?" His eyes shifted to hers and she gasped. "I'm flattered."

"Really?"

"Oh, yeah. This is amazing." He studied it again. "Why did you draw my face?"

"It was just, kinda… stuck in my mind." She knew she sounded childish, but it was the truth. She bit down on her lip to keep it from trembling.

"Wow." He was smiling. "Are you going to finish painting it?"

"I don't know, I…"

"I'll buy it from you. My mother would flip if I sent this to her for her birthday."

Cautiously she moved toward him. Her body began to tingle as she neared him. What was it about the man that made her body tense, her words freeze, and her heart pump so rapidly?

"I've never drawn a face like that from memory. Do you really think it looks like you?" She turned her head to see him staring dumbfounded back at her. "I guess it does."

"How much?"

"I'm sure we could work something out. I've never actually commissioned a portrait before. I usually save those for people I love." The words had flown from her lips before she could retract them. "I didn't mean I was in love with you. I only meant..."

"I know," he reassured her. "For your family."

"Yes."

"I'd be honored if you'd finish it for me. I'm a bit stunned to see myself staring at me." He was at least smiling and she took it as a good sign.

"You don't think it's stalkerish?" There was a feeling brewing in her she wasn't sure she liked. She'd looked at birds and plants and successfully painted them. But having painted a man's face, one who didn't know she was creating his likeness, felt a bit sly.

Trevor stood back from the painting and crossed his arms over his broad chest. "I'll be honest with you. Since I met you yesterday I haven't been able to get you off my mind." He shifted his eyes to the painting. "And I guess I've been on your mind."

"Guilty." She felt the heat rise in her cheeks.

"And my walking into your store this morning was a sign I guess."

"An enormous one."

"So maybe I should let you get to know your subject better. Have dinner with me."

She stared at him, her eyes wide. "Dinner?"

"You do eat, don't you?"

"Yeah." She let out a nervous laugh. "I most certainly do. Okay, I'll go to dinner with you," she said, tucking her shaking hands into the pockets of her jeans.

"I'll pick you up here. When do you close?"

"I'll lock the door at six thirty."

"Great, I'll come back then." He moved toward her. "I'm glad I stopped in to see your brother-in-law."

"Me too." He was so close the scent of his cologne washed over her. She could move in, kiss him, and melt into a pool of goo in the floor, but she resisted. Love, or lust, at first sight wasn't realistic and Hope was much too practical for that.

Trevor smiled at her and walked back through the store.

"Hey," she called out to him. "I don't pick up men in the cemetery, by the way. I just thought I'd let you know."

"I don't usually go looking for women there either. Unless they're my aunt." He winked and left her alone with just his scent in the air and his sketched face staring back at her.

Trevor pulled away from the curb and beat his hand against the steering wheel. He'd just asked her out on a date. He certainly was taking his assignment to heart this time. Get to know her better, he reminded himself of Donald Buchanan's instructions.

"Guess that's what I'm doing," he said to himself as he headed back toward his hotel room to compile the information he'd gathered. A knot of guilt twisted in him. Donald Buchanan was asking him to stalk her. He'd never really thought of his investigating that way, but now that he'd been affected by Hope's charm, he wasn't feeling very good about it at all.

As he walked through the lobby the woman at the front desk called to him. "This came for you today, sir."

He stepped up to the counter and she handed him a thick manila envelope. He waited until he was in the elevator before opening it. As the door closed and he felt the lift of the cage, he unfastened the flap and looked inside the envelope.

"Holy shit."

He was glad he was alone.

Tucked inside were six thousand dollars, in cash, and a note.

Mr. Jacobs:

As per our earlier conversation, please accept this as a good faith offering that I will indeed pay you any price for finding my daughter and getting to know her before I meet her. As you can see this amount is equal to what I've already paid you, and I assure you, I will double this when I have met Hope. I would like you to use this money to cover your extended expenses in Kansas City and shower my daughter with gifts. Though I am not ready to disclose myself to her, someday she will know these gifts have come from me. For the time being, please use the money to see that she is happy.

Sincerely, Donald Buchanan.

Trevor forced himself to take a deep breath and then when he felt lightheaded he realized he'd been holding it. The woman of his dreams had become his assignment. He'd already started the process of getting to know her better when he hadn't revealed himself to her at the cemetery. Then he'd asked her to dinner, because Donald Buchanan had told him to get to know her. Now he was to buy her lavish things.

He slid the key into his door and entered. His life seemed almost perfect. What more could he want? He had a date with the perfect woman, and her biological father was happy to foot the bill. It was as if your prom date's father handed over the keys to his new car. That had never happened, but he assumed this would be how it felt. But then again he wasn't sure an openly offered courtesy would leave a bad taste in your mouth like the offer Donald Buchanan was making did.

"You've been busy today," Hope called from the back when she heard the bells chime over the door at noon. It was no surprise that Thomas appeared in her back room seconds later. It was their routine that he would come by on his lunch break.

"Yeah, lots of new talent today."

"Is that what you call it?" She laughed and he followed suit as he leaned against the doorjamb and watched her work.

She lifted her eyes over the canvas and he gave her a smile that she'd become accustomed to. He was proud of her and just a bit overprotective, which had him checking in on her several times during the day.

"Working on a masterpiece?"

"A commissioned masterpiece, thank you very much."

"Ah, nothing like someone wanting to pay you before you've done all the work."

"Exactly." She swished her sable brush in the jar of solvent to her side then wiped the bristles on a rag and set it on the table.

"Can I look?" He playfully raised his golden brows at her and she sighed, crinkling up her nose.

"Yeah, you can look."

Hope stepped to the side and let Thomas slide in between her and the canvas.

"Mr. Jacobs?" She winced when she nodded. "You've done this much today? He just was in the school this morning. He came over here next?"

"Yes, but I started this yesterday."

"I didn't realize he'd been in here before." He raised his eyes to meet hers, and resentment poked at her when she realized Thomas was uncomfortable with the situation.

"He hadn't," she said on a sigh and reached for a rag to wipe the paint smudges from her hands. "I met him at the cemetery yesterday."

"Carissa said she found you there."

"Found me? She knew I was there." She smiled, pulled open the mini refrigerator, and pulled out a bottle of water. "Want one?"

"I'm good, thanks."

Hope nodded and opened the bottle. She took a long pull, hoping to gather her thoughts about Trevor Jacobs. It was organizing the thoughts that was giving her problems.

Thomas gave her a look of impatience. "Anyway, you met him at the cemetery?"

"Yeah. After Carissa left, I was still standing over Mandy's grave and he walked up. He was looking for his aunt."

"That's some pick-up line." He was smiling, but she knew he was being protective.

"C'mon, who picks up women in the cemetery?"

"Just seems odd that a man meets you in the cemetery and then finds you at work."

"Well now you're creeping me out." She picked up the rag she'd wiped her hands on and threw it at him.

"I'm supposed to look out for you. I've been doing it most of your life."

"Thank you, in case I forget."

"Smart-ass," he said throwing the rag back in her direction. "Seriously, did he know you were an artist? He asked you at the cemetery to do this?" He motioned to the portrait.

"No, actually I started the picture before he asked for it." She walked over to the canvas and stood next to Thomas. "I know this sounds strange, but I couldn't forget his face. It was cluttering my head. I had to sketch it. I had to get it out of there."

"And he just happened to come in here today and see it?"

"Yep, that's how it worked."

Thomas considered it, but she could see it wasn't settling. He frowned. "It's creeping me out now."

"Stop!" She slapped his arm. "Truth is I feel as though I've been waiting for him. As if he was supposed to come for me. Grandma Katie said he would."

"You're talking to Katie? I think you need some fresh air."

"I walk with her in my dreams." She dropped her shoulders. "I know, I know. It sounds strange." Hope looked up at him and let out a breath. "Do you believe in fate?"

Thomas didn't answer right away. He tunneled his fingers through his hair. Hope knew this meant he was thinking, it was one of those unique habits that made Thomas so endearing.

"I guess I'd be a hypocrite if I said I didn't. We all take certain paths for certain reasons, and sometimes they lead us right to the thing we wanted most."

"Had you not run away, you'd never have met my mom and she'd never have led you to Carissa."

"Right. Just think, if your mom hadn't left your dad and toured for ten years I wouldn't have met her either. It seems like your mother's stubbornness was to my benefit." He pursed his lips and gave her a thoughtful nod. "So you think his finding you in the cemetery, your painting his face, and his walking in the door are all fate driven?"

Hope shrugged. "I don't know what to think. But I know his face fills my mind. When we touch there's electricity."

"Touch?" His eyes opened wide.

"We've shaken hands," she said with raised brows.

"Oh." He sighed in a big brother sort of way.

"I guess I'll see what happens tonight."

"Tonight?"

"He's asked me out for dinner."

"And you're going?"

"Creeping you out again?" she asked as she picked up the brush she'd cleaned earlier and tapped it into a dab of Prussian blue for the background.

He touched her arm. "Be careful."

"I've never been anything but."

"I know. I just have a very uneasy feeling about this." He kissed her on the cheek.

"You would. You're supposed to protect me, right?"

"Yeah, me and that medal you wear around your neck." He gave a nod toward her necklace.

Hope touched the pendant. "It did okay by Mom and Carissa. It'll keep me safe."

Thomas gave her a wave goodbye and headed back to the school.

Hope lifted the Saint Nicholas medal from her neck and examined it. Her grandmother had given it to her mother when she was a child. Soon after, they'd been in a car accident and her mother was the only survivor. The accident had taken Sophia's parents from her, scarred her physically, and made her barren. When she'd decided to marry David, she'd given the necklace to Carissa as an engagement present. Carissa, in turn, had given it to Hope when she was ten, shortly after their great-grandma Katie had passed away.

Hope had faith it would keep her safe, but she wasn't sure she'd need it. Trevor Jacobs didn't creep her out. On the contrary, he got her very excited about many things.

As promised, Trevor Jacobs walked through the door to Hope's store just as she was ready to lock up.

She gestured to her faded jeans. "I didn't give much thought to this. I haven't even been able to go home and change."

"I think you look great."

She looked him over. His dark blue jeans and button-down shirt put her at ease. This was going to be casual. She quietly blew out a breath as she thought of the night ahead. It wasn't creeping her out. On the contrary, she was growing more and more excited with the possibilities of what the night would bring.

He led her to the car and opened the door for her after she'd locked up. Luckily, she'd always kept makeup and grooming essentials at the store. She'd had a few moments before he'd gotten there to freshen up. A splash of perfume hadn't hurt either. After all, she'd been working with paint all day.

He pulled the car from the curb. "I saw a place on my way over here this morning. Josephine's? Ever eaten there?"

"I've been known to dine there a time or two."

"Any good?"

"You won't find better. Jo makes your dining experience just that. An experience you won't forget."

"Jo? You've been there more than a time or two, haven't you?"

She laughed. "Yeah. She makes that very thin kind of pizza you find in Italy. Not the thick American kind we know and love. So Thomas would take me there often when I was growing up."

He shifted in his seat. "You and Thomas are pretty close?"

"Very. He was my first love." She felt him shift his eyes from the road to her and she met them with a smile. "I was eight."

He nodded and turned his eyes back toward the road. "Does he know you felt this way?"

"Yes. He knows. He was crazy about my sister and I was crazy about him. I got over it in time and when they got married, I realized how lucky I was. I had a sister and a brother to look after me. By the time I was fourteen, I was an aunt with a baby to play with and then they just kept knocking them out. Now they have four beautiful children that I get to spoil and send home."

"You like kids?"

"I love them." She settled her eyes on him. "Do you?"

"Yeah. My sister has kids. She married young and started right away. She's got two and one on the way."

"Boys or girls?"

"One of each. She's keeping the newest addition a surprise, which is killing my mother. She'd like to know what kind of quilt to make the baby. My sister says make it neutral, but my mom wants to personalize it. It's how she is."

"I think that's lovely."

"Well for now it's just keeping my mother off of my back. I can't tell you how annoying it is to repeatedly be asked when I'm going to give her some grandbabies."

The air thickened in the car. Hope bit down on her lip as she tried to control an emotion that stirred through her when he said those words.

"So where is home?" Hope moved the conversation in the necessary personal direction so she could get to know her date better.

"Upstate New York. Born and raised there, but it's really not my style."

"Really? What's your style?"

"I like city, not country. But I don't like big city. Manhattan is not for me. However, I do a lot of business there, my office is there. But Kansas City is a nice pace. It's big, but it's not." He shook his head. "Does that even make sense?"

"Perfect sense."

Trevor pulled the car into the parking lot and hurried around the car to help Hope out.

"Thank you," she said softly, reaching for his hand. When she touched it, she felt the energy surging again. Only this time it wasn't shocking, it was warm and comfortable. The tightening in her stomach increased.

He took her hand in his, interlacing their fingers, and led them through the front door of the dimly lit restaurant.

She chose a lighter dish of pasta and a white wine sauce. Trevor tried his hand at Jo's signature lasagna.

"Now that's what I'm talking about," he said cheerfully as the dish was set down before him. The slice was the size of the plate.

"Quite the appetite?"

"The company of a beautiful woman does that to me." His gaze had shifted from the plate of pasta and meat to her, and she felt a lump form in her throat. His dark eyes seemed to sparkle over the candlelight. She wondered if it was possible to lose one's heart in less than one day.

"Thank you."

Trevor lifted his glass of red wine. "A toast to new friendships."

Hope tapped her glass to his. "To new friendships."

She sipped her wine and picked up the conversation they'd had in the car. She wasn't finished learning about Trevor Jacobs, the boy from upstate New York.

"So why are you in Kansas City?" she asked as she wrapped noodles around her fork. "Business."

She nodded. Losing her heart to the stranger she'd seen in her dreams seemed like a lost cause. He'd be leaving. That's what it meant when business brought you to Kansas City.

"I probably should have asked before, but what do you do? You certainly aren't the art dealer I pray every morning will walk through my door and buy up all my art." She lifted her glass in a toast again. "Though you did make my month by wanting to purchase my current work."

Trevor lifted his glass too. "I look forward to acquiring my latest purchase." His smile stopped her with her mouth open. Her heart did a little flip and she thought back to the moment when he said he was there on business.

"So, back to why you're in Kansas City."

"Ah." He set his glass back down. "I'm an insurance investigator." He wiped his lips with his napkin and laid it back in his lap.

Hope watched him carefully. He wasn't completely comfortable with his answer. "You don't like your job?"

"What? No, I love it. Insurance is the bread and butter. But for fun I dabble in the personal. Meaning I do some"—he lifted his brow—"PI work," he whispered.

Hope smiled. "Oh."

"The deadbeat dad that needs to be found. The cheating wife. The stealing employee."

Hope looked down at her plate with a nod and then lifted her eyes back to him. "The missing parents?"

"It would fit into my menu of services." Trevor sat back and continued his assault on his lasagna, but Hope suddenly wasn't hungry anymore. She chewed on her bottom lip.

Just the day before, while standing at Mandy's grave, she'd wondered who she was and where she'd come from. Who were the people who created her life and gave her to the wonderful people she called her parents? What kind of blood ran through her? Was Mandy only some coke addict who'd had affairs and gotten knocked up? Was there anything sincere about the woman? Who was the man she'd had an affair with?

Trevor reached across the table and set his hand on hers. "Are you all right?"

Hope snapped back to the conversation. "Yes, sorry."

"You're not eating."

"I'm not really hungry. If you don't mind, I'll save this for lunch tomorrow."

He nodded, wiped his mouth, and then sipped his wine, all the while keeping his eyes focused on her. She caught his stare. She wanted to ask him to help her. She wanted to see if he would, but she needed to talk to Carissa. This would affect her too. After all, the only blood bond she had to the family that raised her was Carissa. They were sisters in blood.

"You don't look so well. Would you like me to take you back to the store to get your car?"

"I'm sorry, Trevor." She settled her eyes into his. Again, her stomach was flipping and her heart was racing. "Would you mind?"

His brows drew together as he studied her for a moment. He gave her a nod, set his napkin on the table, and gave her a noticeably forced smile. "Not at all."

Chapter Three

The waitress boxed up their dinners and the cream-filled cannolis that Trevor ordered. He took Hope's hand and escorted her back to the car.

The ride back was quiet and he began to wonder what he'd said to upset her. Anxiety fluttered in his chest. He hadn't revealed himself to her as someone sent to find her. He would usually have done that by now if he were being on the up-and-up. Instead, he was wining and dining her on her birth father's money. But that was the assignment, he reminded himself with a trickle of guilt; because he really would rather get to know her on his own.

He'd never had an assignment that had gotten so personal. They weren't supposed to. By not backing away he was jeopardizing everything Donald Buchanan wanted from him, only Buchanan was the very man asking him to stay and to be quiet.

He turned his head to catch the glimpse of the angel seated beside him. Maybe she suspected. Maybe she didn't trust him. He hadn't lied to her. He'd only not told her his reason for coming to Kansas City was to find her. He indeed was an insurance investigator. And finding dead mistresses and illegitimate daughters was much more intriguing that hunting down the truth behind a hit-and-run in a parking lot.

Trevor stopped the car in front of her darkened shop. Only one car remained on the street, and it was hers.

Hope turned her head toward him. Her eyes danced in the darkness under the illumination of the street lamp. "Thank you. I had a wonderful time."

"I hope so." He covered her hand with his. "I hope you're feeling better."

"I'm sure I will be."

"I'd like to see you again. Would you mind if I came by tomorrow?" He lifted her fingers to his lips and brushed a kiss over her knuckles. "To check the progress of my acquisition, that is." He let a gentle smile settle on his lips, still lingering over the skin of her hand. He didn't want to let go. The urge to lean forward, kiss her passionately on her rosebud lips, and say to hell with Donald Buchanan was too strong though. He slowly let go of her hand and she pulled it back to her lap.

"Of course."

"And then if you're not busy maybe we could get some coffee?"

"I can't leave the store in the middle of the day," she reminded him.

"Okay then, I'll bring coffee."

"I think that sounds lovely." She reached for the handle of the door.

"Wait." Trevor jumped from the car and ran to the other side. He opened the door, took her hand, and helped her out of the car. "My mother would never forgive me if I just dropped you and drove off. A gentleman makes sure to help a lady from the car, and he waits on the curb to make sure she's gotten her keys in the door. In the case of her driving off, he must wait to see that the car starts and she has driven off."

"I love your mother already."

"She'd love you as well," he said, without realizing how sentimental it would sound.

"Again, thank you. I'm sorry to call it such an early night."

"No worries." He leaned in and kissed her on the cheek. "I'll see you tomorrow."

She smiled at him and walked toward her car. Once she'd opened the door she shot him back another smile. The door shut. The car started and Hope Kendal drove away.

Trevor sprawled out across the bed and reached for his messenger bag. Pulling out the folder that housed the documents he'd collected for the Mandy Marlow case, he eased back and sat against the pillows.

Trevor needed to see Hope's face again. He needed to imagine that it was him she was smiling at when he went to sleep.

He opened it up past the only picture he had of Mandy and Donald and flipped through until he found her.

"I miss you already," he said with a shake of his head. "This is going too far, too fast." He ran his fingers over the picture and remembered how deep the blue of her eyes was. Her smile, her laugh, her voice all haunted him, just as they had in his dreams.

He tossed laid the folder on the nightstand and rearranged the pillows. He prayed Hope Kendal would be in his dreams again tonight.

Hope knocked on Carissa's front door at half past seven the next morning. It took all she had not to laugh at her sister's harried appearance.

"Dear God, Hope! What are you doing here? What happened? Are you all right?" Carissa assaulted her with questions as she pulled her though the door.

"I need to talk to you."

"If you're not injured and no one is dead, can it wait till I get to work? I'm getting breakfast ready. I have three half-naked kids running around and one completely naked one. Thomas had a meeting at the high school, and I have to get them on the bus."

"I'll help you. Give me a task."

An hour later, the house was quieter and everyone was wearing clothes. Carissa set the little ones in front of the television with a movie and sat down with Hope at the table. Hope poured them each a cup of coffee, aware that Carissa was watching her every move.

"Okay, let's talk. Is this about your date with some guy you met at the cemetery, and he walked into your school?"

"Thomas squealed?"

"Like a pig. What did he do?"

Hope laughed. She knew Carissa would never stop being the worrywart big sister.

"He was a perfect gentleman. He's commissioned a painting," she said, leaving out the fact that she'd already started it after having his face etched in her mind.

"Nice, at least he's good for some money."

"Yeah." She let out a little laugh and sipped her coffee. "But that's not what I wanted to talk about. I want to hire him."

"Him? What does he do?"

"He's an insurance investigator."

"And someone hit your car?" Carissa's forehead wrinkled up, causing Hope to smile.

"No. But he finds people."

"And who did you lose?"

"Me."

Carissa sat back and Hope chewed on her lip. Her sister was processing it. She just hoped that she'd see Hope's side.

"You know who you are."

"I'm a Kendal. Don't think I don't know that. My parents are your parents. Sophia is my mom. David my dad. You are my sister. I'm not confused."

"But you're not satisfied."

She'd always thought she was, and it was that little part of doubt that twisted her insides in knots. "Don't you ever want to know who she was?"

"I lived with her, remember? I was tossed around like an unwanted puppy. I had to find Dad myself and I was seven. Then she dumped me on him, thank goodness."

Hope felt the bitterness in her sister's words. They'd never talked about Mandy much, and when they did the conversation usually ended controversially like this one had begun. But Hope wanted more.

"Okay, but here's what we don't know, and what I want to know. Who was Mandy Marlow? Where did she grow up? Who are her parents? Do we have cousins? Do I have siblings? Other siblings," she corrected.

"Don't do this, Hope," Carissa warned.

"Your biological father is David Kendal."

"Hope…"

"I want to know where I came from, Carissa. I want to know who she was and I want to know who my father is."

"How are you going to find that out? Dad doesn't even know who he was. She just showed up here pregnant with you."

"I know. But there has to be a trail."

"A trail that is twenty-three years old."

"Fine. I may not be able to find it on my own, but with Trevor's help…"

"You just might find what you are looking for, and it just might hurt you." Carissa stood and poured out her coffee into the sink. "Why can't you just be happy with the way things are?"

"I am happy, and that's why I know I can do this. I can take what is to be offered to me, process it, and still know I'm David and Sophia's daughter. That will never change. But Carissa, I want to know."

Carissa stared down at her, her arms crossed over her chest. The room was silent for a long moment, and then Hope stood.

"It affects you. That's why I came to you."

"You're going to do it no matter what?"

"I am, but I want you on my side. I'm not sure I'll tell Mom and Dad yet, but I want you to know because I think you can help us. You know so much more than I do."

"So even if I say no?"

"I'm still going to ask, but I want you on my side."

Carissa kept her eyes on her sister. As she considered it, Hope noticed the creases around them softened. "She's no saint. I don't want you to get your feelings hurt when you realize what she was." Hope only nodded. Carissa dropped her shoulders and gave a thoughtful shake of her head. "But I once went searching for a parent too, and look what was at the other end."

Hope smiled. "You won a lottery."

"Jackpot," Carissa said, enveloping Hope in her arms. "But I don't want you to hurt them."

"I won't. I just want to know whose blood runs in my veins. I just have to know."

"Then do it. But, Hope…" She pulled back. "Be careful."

"I will."

He hadn't specified a time to stop by the store, but with every shadow that had passed outside the window, Hope looked up, anticipating it would be Trevor.

The portrait was coming along. Having his deep, dark eyes staring back at her wasn't helping the fact that she was desperately awaiting his arrival.

Finally, the door opened and Trevor walked through with a tray of drinks and a large brown paper bag with the word deli printed on it.

"We only discussed having coffee, but I thought since I was late enough, I would bring lunch too. I hope you don't mind."

"I think that's wonderful. Let me help you," she offered as she crossed the store to take the tray of coffees from him. "We can eat at the table in the back."

She set the cardboard cups on the table and he set the bag next to them.

"Would you like to see your acquisition?" She laughed as she turned toward the canvas.

Trevor walked to the easel. He stopped and stared. The artist in her picked up the flash of emotion that glossed over his eyes.

"Oh, Hope. This is amazing."

"Thank you."

"When I give it to her I want you to be there." He turned to her. "I want you to see her face when she looks at it for the first time."

Hope swallowed back the lump in her throat. "That's thoughtful, but..."

"No buts. She's just going to flip."

"C'mon, let's eat. I want to talk to you, but I think I'm going to need a substantial amount of food in me to get through it."

"You're still hungry because you didn't finish your dinner last night. In fact, I had it for breakfast this morning. You left it in the car."

"I'm sorry," she said snorting out a laugh. "How thoughtless of me."

"We'll let it slide." He pulled her chair out for her and then sat down next to her at the small table, pushed up against the wall. "You're feeling better I take it?"

Hope raised her shoulders and let them fall as she unwrapped the sandwich he'd brought her. She seriously was going to need the fuel to make it through the conversation.

"I'm fine. It's just... well, I need to talk to you."

A sliver of a smile crossed his lips as he laid his hand atop of hers. "I know I didn't get you pregnant, I haven't even touched you." He laughed with a wink of his eye and Hope lightened up.

"Sorry to be so dramatic." She pulled back and took a bite of her sandwich. "It's just what I'm about to ask you has the potential to give me the world, or ruin it."

"Well I'd be up for running off to Vegas and getting married too, but do you really think it would ruin you?" He smiled again and she laughed.

"I don't remember you being such a comedian last night."

"I had on my good manners. Now you're seeing me."

"I like it."

He set his sandwich down and settled his eyes into hers. Hope watched as he moved slowly toward her. As he neared, she closed her eyes and felt the warmth of his lips gently brush hers. When she opened her eyes, he was right there.

"You have no idea how happy that makes me."

"Wow. This isn't how I thought this would go," she admitted.

"Wasn't on my agenda either, but I don't mind detours."

"Good, then back to what I needed to ask."

"I'm all ears."

Hope gathered her nerves. Carissa had given her a green light to ask him, but she knew her sister wasn't excited about the venture. The fear that she might hurt her parents by pursuing her past made her nauseated. Her stomach churned and the rate of her heart kicked up, but she took a breath and began.

"Would you be interested in helping me find out about my birth parents?"

It was out. She'd posed the question. His dark eyes shot wide open and he almost choked on his lunch. Quickly, he'd sipped his coffee and stood. His reaction wasn't what she'd expected.

He paced back and forth all the while her heart rate picked up speed. "You want to find your birth parents?"

She nodded.

"You said your birth mother was buried at the cemetery."

"She is. But I don't know any more than that. Well, not a lot more, and I have no idea who my birth father is."

He scrubbed his hands over his face and Hope stood to face him. "Listen, if you don't want to help me, I understand. I just thought, since this is what you do and all. It's not like I'm asking for a favor. I'd pay you whatever your cost is. I just…"

"Hope." He touched her arm and she calmed. "Are you sure you want to do this? Are you sure you want to know about these people who gave you up?"

"He didn't give me up, she did. And don't get me wrong, I'm grateful for the family I have. I just want to know who they were."

He nodded. "Okay. Let me see what I can find, and we'll start there."

"Oh, Trevor, thank you." She wrapped her arms around his neck. "I appreciate this so much."

He held her back just far enough that she could see his face clearly.

"Prepare yourself. It could be long journey and one you may not be ready for."

"I'm ready. Thank you. Thank you." She kissed him on the cheek.

Trevor'd hoped to spend more of the day with Hope, but after she'd asked for his help, he couldn't sit so close to her. He felt as though he was betraying her, but how could he be? He had been sent there to do a job, and he'd done his job. He'd found Mandy Marlow and he'd found her daughter. The only problem was, he was sure he was falling for Hope and that wasn't going to help. He needed to get in touch with Donald Buchanan as soon as possible. Hope wanted to meet her birth father and Trevor knew where to find him. And where did that leave him? As soon as Hope found out he'd been following her, she was surely not going to trust him anymore. Why would she? He was a paid stalker. God, what if she found out about the money Donald Buchanan had sent him to spend on her?

Trevor paced his hotel room, running his fingers over his hair. He was a fraud and should be in jail! Which was what he figured would happen as soon as David Kendal found out what he'd done.

"What a mess you're in." He scolded himself in the mirror on the dresser. "This is not going to work."

His cell phone buzzed on the table. He scooped it to his ear. "Jacobs here."

"Mr. Jacobs, it's Donald Buchanan. I wanted to make sure you received the package I sent for you."

He tossed a glance toward the bed where the envelope still sat, and a tingle ran through him. "Yes, sir, I did."

"Good. Please use it on her and make her happy. I want her to be happy."

"Yes, sir." Trevor gathered his thoughts and cleared his throat. "Sir, I was just wondering, are you considering a meeting with your daughter anytime soon?"

"Not yet. My wife knows I'm up to something. I can't let her know about Hope." That was pretty typical of a parent seeking an illegitimate child. Buchanan drew in a sharp breath. "Perhaps this isn't the nicest thing to say about my own wife, but... I fear for Hope's safety should my wife find out about her."

"Then why did you send me here?" Anger rose in his voice. The feeling of caretaker and protector had again taken over.

"I beg your pardon?"

"Sir, with all due respect, why find her if you are afraid your wife would harm her? Why would you put her in danger?"

"Perhaps you've forgotten your place, Mr. Jacobs. You were paid to find her."

"And now I'm being paid to get to know her, remember."

"Of course. That doesn't mean you should get emotionally invested in her."

"Well, I'd say that's too late." He shook his head and cursed himself silently for saying that.

"Mr. Jacobs, is there something going on between you and my daughter?"

"No, sir. We are becoming friends." He left it at that.

"Well then, I know you will take good care of her. I won't hold off much longer. My wife will be leaving the country to vacation with her sister soon. I think that would be the best opportunity for us to meet."

"As long as you feel it's safe." He was very glad he hadn't given Donald Buchanan more information on Hope. But then again, it wouldn't have been too hard for him to find either.

"Yes, I believe it will be. Thank you, Mr. Jacobs, we will talk soon."

The line went dead.

Trevor fell back onto the bed. He thought about what Hope had asked him to do. She wanted to find out about her parents. It was doable and she deserved that much. They'd start with Mandy. They could build on that and then... Then, depending on what Donald Buchanan wanted to do, he'd steer her toward him. However, if Donald Buchanan thought Trevor would get careless enough to let his wife get her hands on Hope, he was wrong. Trevor was going to protect her. He'd never run a case like this before, never gotten so personal, and he'd never felt like he did for anyone before he met Hope. She'd been the woman of his dreams. He wasn't going to let anything happen to her.

Hope opened the store. She hadn't seen Trevor in two days. Her heart ached. Perhaps he wasn't who she thought he was. She'd asked for his help. He'd panicked and now he'd disappeared.

She stared at his face on the canvas. The dark eyes that had her blood pumping so swiftly stared up at her. She'd seen his face before, she was sure of it. He'd been there when she slept, in her dreams. This was the face she'd become so familiar with.

The painting would only need a few more brushstrokes and it would be finished.

"You back there?" Thomas's voice rang through the store, though it was still early in the day.

"Yes."

He poked his head around the wall and smiled. "You've been kinda quiet the past few days. I just thought I'd check in. I have orchestra practice in a few minutes so I'll be tied up."

"Is this beginning orchestra?" She scrunched up her nose.

"Yes, and when you hear flat notes, know I've sent those to you special."

She laughed. She deserved that. "I've been warned."

"I haven't seen Trevor around."

She nodded. She'd known he had a reason for stopping by. "No. I asked him to help me find out about my parents, and I haven't seen him since."

Thomas nodded. She knew Carissa wouldn't have kept it a secret. "Maybe he's investigating."

"Maybe."

The bell on the door chimed, and Thomas turned to see who had walked through the door. "Speak of the devil."

Hope's mouth went dry and her stomach tightened. She wiped her hands on the rag that hung from the easel and walked past Thomas.

"Hi." Her voice was light.

"Sorry I haven't called. I had some business to take care of. But I brought you this." He handed her a manila envelope.

Her eyes didn't leave his as he handed it to her.

Thomas cleared his throat. "Well, I have to go make music. Trevor, it was nice to see you again." He turned to walk back through the store.

"Mr. Samuel, I'm sorry. I didn't see you there." Trevor straightened his posture.

"It's Thomas." Trevor nodded. Thomas turned back to Hope. "I'll send Carissa over when she gets time."

"I'll see her soon, then."

Thomas kissed her on the cheek and headed out the door.

"Sorry. I shouldn't have done that in front of him," Trevor apologized.

She only shook her head. Words weren't coming to her. She could only imagine what was in the envelope, but even more, she'd missed him. "Can I get you something to drink?"

"I'd love a bottle of water if you have one."

Hope walked to the back room. She opened the little refrigerator and pulled out a bottle of water. When she turned to hand it to him, she found he was in front of the painting.

"This is amazing."

"Thank you."

"It gets better every time I see it."

"Here." She handed him the bottle.

"Thanks." Their eyes met briefly, and then his shifted back to the painting.

"End of August. Can you go with me?"

Hope laughed. "I'm sorry. What's the end of August?"

"Mom's birthday. I want to give this to her and I still want you there."

"Oh." Hope turned, but he caught her arm.

"I know you're upset because I disappeared for a few days."

"Why should I be upset? We had a few meals together, that's all. You're commissioning me to paint you, and I've offered to commission you to find some information. I guess you've done your part." She motioned toward the envelope with her hand. "And I've done mine." She gave a nod to the painting.

"I think you know there is more here," he said, and she could feel tears stinging her eyes.

"Do you think so?"

"Hope." He cupped her face in his hands. "I want there to be."

Her mouth dropped open and she gave a gasp, but then his mouth found hers. Her body swayed toward him as his lips parted and his tongue sought hers. There wasn't time to dissect what she was doing. She knew what it was. She was falling for a man she'd only met, and she couldn't seem to help herself. But then again, it was only physically that they'd just met. In her dreams, she'd known him much longer.

Hope raised her arms around his neck as Trevor slid his hands down her sides. Her head spun with the delight of his lips. Her heart raced. Her body tingled as he touched her ever so lightly.

Trevor pulled back and rested his forehead against hers. "I was so afraid you wouldn't even talk to me today."

"I missed you," she said honestly.

"I missed you too."

They stood silent, letting the moment wash over them.

"C'mon. Let's sit down and look at what I brought you." He stepped back and pulled the chair out for her.

Hope nodded, but her entire body stiffened. She'd said she could handle everything that she found out. Now was the real test. Could she indeed handle it?

She sat and so did Trevor. He slid the envelope toward her and moved his chair closer.

Her fingers trembled as she lifted the flap and pulled out the contents.

Chapter Four

Trevor watched Hope as she picked through the papers. This was only a quarter of the information that he'd pulled together from his findings on Mandy Marlow. It had taken him two days to shuffle through his own paperwork to find part of what she was looking for. He'd wanted to give her a profile of a woman she wouldn't want to find. If Hope saw the worst of Mandy Marlow first, maybe she'd decide to forget finding out about her altogether.

"This doesn't paint a very pretty picture, does it?" Hope held up a mug shot of her birth mother. Her face was swollen and bruised, and the information that followed said she'd been in a fight at a bar.

Trevor looked at the picture she held. He had wanted to show her the negative first with hopes she would abandon the thought of digging up more information. "The dates indicate she must have been about thirty there."

"She was only thirty-four when I was born. My dad said she was clean when she was pregnant with me."

Trevor shrugged. He didn't have those answers. Not yet.

Hope sifted through pictures in the pile. They were copies of what Trevor had in his file.

"I've only seen pictures of her a few times. My dad once said I looked just like her, but I don't see it."

Trevor looked at the picture and then at Hope. "No, you don't look like that woman at all, but your dad obviously saw her differently once."

"I don't think so. All I know is they had this brief affair. She was young and he was stupid, he said." She laughed. "When you meet my dad you'll laugh too. He's such a wise man, I don't know how he ever got involved with someone like Mandy Marlow."

"Men as a rule aren't very bright," he said, hoping she wouldn't realize he fit into that category.

"Some of you seem okay."

His heart slammed into his ribs and he had to rub his chest to keep it from bursting through. How was he going to help her with this, knowing that in the end she'd just hate him for keeping secrets?

"What has your dad told you about her?"

Hope sat back in her chair. "I've never done too much asking. I didn't want to hurt anyone. But they never kept my adoption secret." She leaned forward again, her arms rested on the table. Her eyes went soft and a soft smile formed on her lips. "My mother has a plaque on her wall that has a poem about adoption. I asked when I was little what it meant and she told me that someone else had given Carissa and me to her to be her very own. She was so gracious, and it must have hurt like hell to have me ask." Hope reached for Trevor's hand and interlaced their fingers. "My mom couldn't have her own children. She'd been in a car accident when she was just a little girl. Her parents died in the accident and she was left with scars and injuries. One of those injuries made her barren."

"She sounds like quite a woman."

"She is. She's a survivor." Hope's eyes misted. "I know it couldn't have been easy. She'd left my dad before they were married because of Carissa. She thought my dad purposely didn't tell her he had a child. Truth was, he didn't know Carissa existed. He thought he'd left Mandy and moved on with his life. Then my sister showed up at their door, said, 'I'm your daughter,' and my mom left."

Hope ran her hands through the papers on the table again, spreading them out, glancing over them. "Mom had a wonderful career as a concert cellist in Europe, but when she finally came back ten years later, she learned the truth. She and Carissa fell in love and so did she and dad. Then Mandy showed back up.

"Every time she'd gotten close to marrying my dad, Mandy always showed back up."

"This time with another baby," he said on a sigh as if he realized what an amazing man David Kendal was for taking Hope and giving her a home.

"Oh, and not just a baby, no, she's going to die too." Hope shook her head, her blonde curls swayed over her shoulders. "I was in the NICU for three weeks when I was born."

"NICU?"

"Neonatal intensive care unit." She shifted her eyes to him. "Mandy died as I was being born."

"Hope…"

"I'm not sad. I'm grateful." She laughed. "That sounds bad. I'm not grateful that she died. I'm grateful that for once in her short, miserable life, she made a wise decision. She gave me to a woman who wanted a baby and loved me so much. She gave me to my father, who is simply the most amazing man to walk the earth. Then she gave me my biological sister. What a gift."

Trevor reached for her hand and gave it a squeeze. "So why do this, then? Why dig up what you know will be hurtful to you?" He picked up the mug shot and looked it over. "Hope, this is bound to only get worse."

"I'm strong enough to know I'm a Kendal, not a Marlow. You will never see me in a mug shot like this." She took the photo from him, looked it over, and then tossed it back on the pile. "I am an artist. I am a business owner," she said, swinging her arms through the air to emphasize what she'd built. "I'm more than Mandy Marlow's discarded daughter."

"You're amazing."

"Thank you. And thank you for doing this. Just tell me what I owe you and we'll settle up."

"I think you owe me a dinner that you'll eat." He touched her cheek and she smiled.

"Okay. I'll even cook. No expense out of your pocket."

"Sounds great."

"Let me find a pen and I'll write down my address. I close at six thirty. Don't even think about showing up until about eight. I'll need that much time. I'm not a good cook."

"So is this some kind of punishment?"

"You can be the judge of that."

"I can't wait," he said as he leaned in and kissed her softly on the lips.

Later when he drove away from her shop he wondered if he'd been successful in letting her see the dark side of Mandy Marlow. Would she pore over the pictures and papers and realize it wasn't worth pursuing further? For the moment he hoped she'd hold off, at least until Donald Buchanan came forward.

Trevor sat in his car outside of Hope's apartment. This time it was different. He'd be walking through the door as a welcomed guest.

He opened the mirror on the visor and checked his face. Suddenly he was afraid he'd missed a spot when shaving. He'd applied the same cologne he wore every day, but now he wondered if he'd used too much. He fixed the one hair that seemed out of place, which was hard when he had such short hair.

Next to him was a bouquet of daisies. He'd snuck into the music school and asked Thomas what he should buy her. He had been assured that all of the Kendal women adored daisies as far back as Sophia's grandmother and David's aunt.

He checked his watch. "Eight o'clock on the dot," he assured himself as he reached for the flowers, climbed from the car, and walked across the street.

As he placed his finger on the doorbell, the door flew open.

"You are worse than a woman. Do you know that?" Hope wrapped her arms around his neck and gave him a quick peck on the lips.

"Were you watching me?"

"You pulled up at seven forty-six. You fixed your hair in the mirror, messed with the buttons on the radio, sniffed the front of your shirt," she said with a laugh. "Then finally after checking your watch you made your appearance."

"I didn't know I was a show." He swallowed the lump of guilt and fear that had bundled themselves in his throat.

He'd watched Hope, much like she'd watched him. Intimate details, much like the ones she'd given him, had been written down in a notebook. It was an uncomfortable feeling to be faced with it. But he had to remind himself it was his job. How would she see it though, he wondered.

She kissed him again. "I enjoyed it."

Hope stepped back and he handed her the daisies. "I have it on good authority you like daisies."

"Thomas?"

"Guilty," he confessed.

"You went out of your way, didn't you?" She studied him, and his stomach clenched. He didn't want to lose what they were building.

"I'm still working on impressing you."

"It worked." She pulled him into the apartment, kicked close the door, and pulled him to her, disorienting him with sweet taste of her mouth on his.

His hands settled on her hips and moved her toward the wall. Without leaving her mouth, he took the flowers from her hand and laid them on the table next to them. Her arms lifted around his neck and he nudged his hips against hers, deepening the kiss.

As her tongue met his, he wrestled with his conscience. He should come clean. He should tell her he'd followed her and that he knew all about her. Most of all, he should tell her he knew where to find her father and her mother's family.

He pulled back and rested his head against her shoulder. Her fingers moved over his hair as she caught her breath beneath him. His fingers pressed into her hips as he fought for control over his body.

"We'd better stop. Too much more of this and you'll hate me."

She threw back her head and let out a throaty laugh that ignited the heat in his body again and made it hard to not press his body against her more.

"I could never hate you." Her voice was thick and unsteady as she raised her hands to his chest and gripped the front of his shirt.

"Hope." He pulled back to look her in the eye. "You're in charge in this department. I don't think I've hidden my desire for you all that well." He let out a laugh, and the sultry look in her eyes told him she was aware of it too. "But I don't want you doing anything you don't want to do. So, with that said, I hope this continues."

Hope blew out a breath. "You sure are a gentleman, aren't you?"

A gentleman wouldn't keep secrets from the woman who was squeezing his heart.

"I told you, my mother raised me that way." And sometimes it was the very thought of facing the wrath of Violet Jacobs that made him take his lips off a beautiful woman and wait—patiently.

"Remind me to thank her when we see her in August." She picked up the flowers and started toward the kitchen.

He caught her arm. "You'll go?"

She laid her hand on his chest. "You asked me, didn't you?"

"Well, maybe this will continue in the right direction," he said with a wink as she turned from him and walked back to the kitchen.

"Is that the car you've been driving the whole time?" she asked as he followed her. She pulled a vase from a cabinet and filled it with water.

"Yeah, why?" His voice shook. He hoped she didn't notice.

"I swear there was one like that parked out front on my birthday. It was there for an hour, but was gone when I came home from my sister's."

"Birthday?"

"The day I met you." She turned and gave him a smile. "Best present I've gotten in years."

He swallowed hard. She'd seen him. Damn! "Happy birthday." He walked up behind her and placed a kiss on her neck.

"Let's keep that for after dinner, shall we," she said breathlessly. "Help me set the table. Dishes are in that cupboard."

Trevor climbed into bed and adjusted the pillows and blankets to make himself comfortable. It wasn't happening.

He'd made sure to keep his manners intact. He had helped her set the table and clear it when dinner was finished. He dried dishes after she washed them and helped her from her seat on the patio where they had ended up after dessert. Then after a long, deep, and passionate kiss, he'd said good night. He hadn't wanted to leave, but he knew it was in the best interest for all parties.

Donald Buchanan had told him to get to know her, but he hadn't told her to take her to bed. Likewise, Hope was now a client. Business and pleasure were like oil and water. They didn't mix. If you tried, you usually made a mess. But he couldn't help but want to take that relationship between them further. He was willing to throw away the hefty fee that Donald Buchanan had already paid just to be with Hope. And he didn't want to be with her for just a tumble between the sheets. No, there was something more there he wanted to explore. But she was surely going to hate him when she found out why he'd happened upon her at the cemetery. The night was long. He tossed and turned. He'd given her a few leads as to who Mandy Marlow was, but that wasn't going to hold her off until Donald Buchanan decided to come forward. He didn't want her to accidently stumble into Donald Buchanan's wife either. He was walking a tightrope and he knew it. The only answer was to steer her toward the answers she wanted—and remain close enough to protect her.

She'd mentioned that she'd open the store on Saturday at ten and closed by two. He'd be waiting for her with a box of pastries and coffee. Maybe she'd allow him to spend the day with her in her element.

A smile crossed his lips. It was crazy. How could he have let an assignment become so personal? Then the reality kicked in. Eventually he'd have to leave Kansas City and return to New York. He still had a job there. An apartment he was paying for and a roommate who'd called three days ago looking for him.

It would be easy enough to liquidate it all and relocate to Kansas City. He laughed and ran his hands over his hair. Now he knew he'd lost his mind. He'd met Hope Kendal six days earlier and now he was willing to give up all he'd worked for? Then he thought about what she wanted. Essentially, she'd hired him to help her find her birth parents. There was reason to stick around awhile longer.

He blew out a breath. It would all come together. It was just another puzzle and as an investigator, he was the right man to put that puzzle together.

Trevor watched Hope work from the front window of her store. She was helping a customer at the counter, and three others walked through looking at gifts. She caught sight of him and smiled. When he dangled the bag of pastries and held up the tray of coffee, her eyes lit. She pointed to the back of the store and Trevor let himself into the store and walked directly back to the small room with the table while she finished her sale.

It was fifteen minutes and two pastries later that she finally ducked her head into the back room. She didn't say a word to him. Instead she cupped his face in her hands and laid a gentle, warm kiss on his lips.

"Now that's a thank-you." He smiled.

"I missed you."

"I've only been away from you for twelve hours."

"Too long." She sat down across from him and opened the bag he'd brought in with him. "Cherry turnovers. My favorite!"

"Good guess on my part." He popped the last bit of his into his mouth as he watched her take a bite of hers. Her eyes closed as she took her first bite. A purr came from her throat and his closed up. He cleared his throat and tried to clear his mind. "What are you doing after work?"

"I'm going to the recreation center for a swim. Come with me." She shifted her eyes to him as she licked a piece of cherry from the turnover. He adjusted in his chair, finding it very uncomfortable as he watched her enjoy her pastry.

"I didn't pack a suit for my trip." But he was so turned on watching her eat, he wasn't sure being near her in a public place half naked was a good idea.

"Well, you have time to go get one, or I can see if my dad or Thomas has one you could borrow."

Trevor laughed. "I seriously do not think I'm ready to be borrowing clothes from your family members." He reached his hand to her hair and slipped her blond curls through his fingers. Tracing the loop of a curl, he followed it to her jaw and let his finger slide toward her chin, enjoying the softness of her skin. "How about I meet you back at your place this evening and take you out to dinner."

"Really, you won't come swim with me?" She batted her eyelashes at him, lowering her head, and letting her bottom lip jut out in a pout.

Trevor cleared his throat again. "Doesn't intrigue me."

"Okay, well then, will you do me a favor?" Hope wrapped her fingers around his hand.

"Anything else."

"Tomorrow at five o'clock go to dinner at my parents' house with me."

The two pastries he'd eaten fell into the pit of his stomach. This was not in his find-Mandy-Marlow-and-get-to-know-Hope-Kendal plan. "Your parents?"

"Yes. I want you to meet them. Besides, it's tradition. We all have dinner at my parents' house on Sunday evening. Thomas will be there. At least you'll know one person." She smiled as she stood and moved to sit on his lap. "It would mean a lot to me."

He wasn't sure he was ready for such a leap, but then again nothing about his week or this assignment seemed to be going the way he'd originally anticipated it.

"Okay. I'll be there."

"Thank you," she squealed as the bell on the front door rang. "My mother is a fantastic cook," she assured him as she started out into the store. "You won't be sorry."

He was already sorry. He took a sip of his coffee and scorched his tongue. As he held his hand over his mouth to ward off his curses, he wondered what he was doing. Meeting her parents involved more people in his quest to get to know her for Donald Buchanan. Once her family was involved, it was going to be even trickier to get her to understand why he hadn't revealed his real intentions. He'd never had a case where his feelings got in the way, as they had with Hope.

Things always got personal, to some extent. As an investigator you usually worked for the person getting screwed over. It was hard, if you had a heart, not to feel a little something for your client. But in Hope's case it was different. He'd never before wanted to stop the pursuit for his own selfish reasons. If he didn't have an outside client wanting him to find Hope and he hadn't agreed to let Hope hire him, he'd have a clear conscious about the relationship they were forming. The money and the pursuit didn't matter anymore. Hope was the only thing that mattered.

This time he took her out for Chinese food. She ate. He considered it a successful date. They'd kissed good night on the front step of her apartment. It was a long good-night kiss too. He'd been a gentleman and declined the invitation into the house when she'd offered. Instead, he opted for the cold shower before bed and an hour of going over his documents pertaining to Mandy Marrow.

He'd decided to give her his information in tiny bits. Still, he needed to keep Hope's discovery of her mother low key until Donald Buchanan wanted to meet her. He'd pulled out a few more copies of photos he'd obtained and a few of the cold leads. He'd give them to Hope on Monday, after he met her parents.

Sunday afternoon he arrived at five o'clock to the house on Cherry Street. According to the directions that Hope had written out for him, the modest home with the large front porch and pots of geraniums was the right place.

From the backyard, he could hear the faint laughter of children playing. Such innocent joy brought a smile to his face as he neared the steps of the house. In his hand he carried daisies and a bottle of Italian wine. All complements of a phone call to Thomas, before he'd left the school on Saturday. Surely he'd have a half a chance with winning over her mother.

Trevor hadn't even made it to the top step when the door flew open. Sophia stood before him, an enormous smile on her face. He'd studied her face from photographs he'd had in his file, and he'd have recognized her anywhere. She pushed open the screen door. "You must be the man we've heard so much about."

"I'm Trevor, Mrs. Kendal. It's nice to meet you. Thank you for having me." He held out the flowers and the wine. "These are for you and this is for dinner. I was told it was your favorite."

Sophia nodded, accepting the gifts. "It's Sophia. I see you have been talking to an informant."

"Guilty."

"I'm impressed. Come in and meet the family," she said as stepped aside to let him through. "Hope will be along in a few moments. She had something come up." She shut the door behind them.

Panic flooded his body. Hope had invited him to dinner and he'd never thought to look for her car out front. He was alone in the house of the very people he'd studied, investigated, and consequently ended up admiring. However, he was facing them alone.

The moment Sophia showed Trevor into the living room, he recognized Hope's father. David Kendal stood and crossed the room. He extended his hand, and Trevor reminded himself to extend his.

"Trevor, it's nice to meet you. I'm David, Hope's father."

He couldn't remember a time when his knees felt weak and his palms got sweaty in a room full of strangers. There had been cases when people had come after him with baseball bats and even one crazy wife with a gun, but meeting Hope's parents seemed to be testing him as a man.

"It's a pleasure to meet you."

"She talked you into dinner at the folks'?" Thomas walked up behind David and held out his hand.

"She did."

"She must like you a lot." He raised an eyebrow. "I don't even recall her inviting anyone before."

"I think you're right. Wait." David turned to his son-in-law. "Oliver. Was that his name? Oliver?"

Trevor felt the pang of jealousy pierce his chest. He rubbed against it with his hand. There was no reason for him to be jealous over Hope brining another man home to meet her parents. Hadn't he brought other women home to meet his mother?

He turned his attention to Thomas, who had begun to laugh.

"Oliver? Did you think they were dating?"

"Weren't they?"

"Oliver is gay. He's an artist who wanted her to help him paint."

Trevor let out a quiet breath and the tension in his chest eased.

David shrugged. "Really? I guess I didn't pay too much attention."

"I sure as hell did," Thomas added. "He asked me for my phone number and then wondered if maybe my wife knew I was gay." He shook his head, and David stifled a laugh. "Just because I'm a pianist doesn't mean I'm gay."

"He did that? Was I here for all of this?" Sophia asked.

"I think I discreetly took care of the situation." Carissa walked up behind them and smiled. "I'm Carissa. It's a pleasure to meet you." She extended her hand and he shook it. "Why don't you come on back? I'll get you a glass of wine."

She took Trevor by the hand and escorted him to the kitchen.

He leaned against the counter as Carissa reached for a glass in the cupboard. "So you're Hope's sister?"

"That's me."

"She's very fond of you."

"I hope so. I'm very fond of her too." Carissa smiled as she handed him a glass of wine. "Dinner is almost done. Why don't we sit out on the porch until she gets here."

Trevor waited for her to take a seat and then sat in the chair next to hers overlooking the manicured yard. There were three children running in the grass, chasing a small dog. Another sat on a tree swing, earphones in his ears, trying his best to ignore his siblings.

"This is a wonderful house."

"It is, isn't it?" Carissa looked around. "My parents bought this house over thirty years ago. They fixed it up and then when mom moved to Europe, Dad sold it and he and I moved. Then when Mom moved back to Kansas City ten years later, my great-grandmother and great-aunt bought it for them as a wedding present. We brought Hope home here after she was born. This is where she grew up."

"You didn't grow up in this house?"

"I was here for a bit. I lived here from the time I was seven until the time I was about nine. Then during my senior year in high school and the first summer I was home from college. But that was about it. I lived with my great-grandmother and aunt as they got on in years. Now I live in that house with my family."

The story seemed nicely tucked into a tidy package, but he knew there was so much more to Carissa's life. Mandy Marlow had all but screwed up all of that, he knew. She'd had Carissa in miscellaneous homes for the first seven years of her life before dumping her on David. Knowing the man now, he was sure it wasn't dumping her on him. But he knew that was why Carissa's mother had moved to Europe for ten years. And to think they'd brought Hope to that very house to grow up. He sipped his drink. Hope, who had been born to a dying woman and taken in by the man she claimed as her father. They could make a movie about how Mandy Marlow's children turned out normal. Thank God for people like David Kendal and his wife, Sophia. Carissa and Hope had normal and loving lives.

Carissa set her glass on the small table between the chairs.

"So, Trevor, where are you from?"

"Oh, I was raised in upstate New York." He sipped his wine again. What was he doing? He was now answering personal questions about himself. Did he need a reminder that no matter what was happening to his heart, Hope Kendal was still an assignment and now a client?

"And you moved out to Kansas City for work?"

"Well, I actually am here on work. I don't live here."

"Oh." Carissa picked up her wine and he could feel the air thicken.

"Are you quizzing my date? Did he pass?" He'd never been more grateful to hear a voice in his life. He turned to see Hope standing a mere three feet away looking as angelic as he'd remembered her on her birthday.

"Yeah, you can keep him," Carissa said coolly as Trevor stood to greet Hope.

"I'm sorry I was late."

"Everything okay?" He kissed her cheek.

"Yeah, remind me to tell you later." She smiled and there was a sparkle in her eye. He wondered what she was up to.

Thomas poked his head out of the back door and motioned for them to come back into the house. "Now that everyone is here, let's eat."

"Thomas is our timekeeper." Hope hugged to Trevor's arm. "Sunday night is his special time with his kids. He gets them their baths and reads them a special story. Most of the time Carissa will stay here for a bit just so she doesn't get in their way. There's a weekly chess game to be had between Dad and me, and then I take her home when she's sure they're ready to be tucked in."

"You all work together to make everything meld, don't you?"

"That's what family is about."

He was glad to hear her say that. He'd seen too many people chase down parents they'd never known only to give up the security of what they'd had—a loving home.

Seated around the table, Trevor realized it had been too long since he'd been home. The last time he'd sat at a table with someone under the age of twenty had been

Thanksgiving, and that was coming up on a year. Hope had at least one meal a week with her family. Trevor began missing his.

His family had always been tight-knit. Or so he'd thought. His parents were in love, and still married to each other. His sister and her husband had a happy family. He'd always assumed the day would come and he'd find the right woman and they'd fit their tidy little family in with the others. Now he was thirty and he'd yet to find that one woman who understood that.

He glanced at Hope.

Perhaps he had found her.

She'd haunted his dreams. She'd been handed to him as an assignment. She'd worked her way into his heart in a matter of a week. Now he sat at the dining room table of her parents, and he felt at home.

Right then and there, he knew he had to come clean. He had to tell Donald Buchanan that he had to come forward or he'd let Hope know all about him. He had to tell her the truth about everything so that she wouldn't think he was deceiving her. If she really wanted to learn about Mandy Marlow, he could tell her. He could take her to meet the people she wanted to meet, but he didn't think she should. He thought she should leave it all alone.

Then again, he knew that was selfish.

The reason he got into investigation was that he couldn't leave well enough alone. If there was a question of doubt, he was the one to find the answer. What bigger doubt could you have than not to know who'd given you life?

"So, Trevor, how long have you been in insurance investigation?" Sophia asked as she began helping Carissa fill the children's plates.

"For about eight years. My mother is in insurance. She's had her own company for most of my life. So I guess you could say I've always been in it."

"And what does your father do?"

"He's a corporate lawyer."

Sophia nodded as she took her seat. "And siblings?"

"I have one sister. She's married with two kids and one on the way."

"Oh, how wonderful." Sophia sighed. "Being a grandmother is so wonderful." She gave her grandson's head a gentle rub. "You think you love all you can when you become a parent, but when they hand you a grandchild to love…" She dabbed at her eye as a tear formed. "Well, it only gets better."

Trevor took a moment to watch David as his wife spoke. He'd smiled though his eyes, that kind of smile that told the world your heart belonged to that special person.

Sophia had done an amazing thing by taking on the role of Carissa's mother and raising Hope. He genuinely wondered if there were times when it slipped her mind that she hadn't actually given birth to them.

"Trevor, how long will you be in Kansas City?" Carissa asked.

Trevor caught the tone. Carissa Kendal didn't trust him. Why should she? "Until my work here is done."

He saw Hope's head dip down, diverting her eyes from the conversation. His stomach was twisting into knots. "But I really like it here. New York is too big. I'm going to give some thought to making a move this way."

Her head came up and he was glad. It was something he'd have to give some serious thought to. He'd been very careful not to lie to Hope or her family. Leaving out details was not lying, he told himself yet again.

"I thought your sister lived here? Or was moving here," Thomas innocently added.

Trevor swallowed hard and smiled. "I would love them to, but she wouldn't think of it until the baby is born."

Thomas nodded and Trevor willed his heart rate to lower. If he survived the evening without hanging by the tree in the yard, he'd call it a success.

Sophia finally sat down and began to eat her meal. "I heard you commissioned a painting from Hope for your mother."

"Yes. I've never seen such talent. She's amazing." He smiled as her eyes settled on his. There was hope that he hadn't completely made an ass of himself.

"I have her first portrait in my office at the house." Thomas's smile showed the pride he had in Hope.

"Yeah, you were a glutton for punishment. First I nearly killed him with my lack of talent for the piano, and then I made him sit for hours and hours so I could attempt to paint him."

"I'd do it all over again," he said with love in his eyes, and Trevor knew that he meant it. He knew Thomas would do anything for Hope, her whole family would. And he'd have to assume that also meant they'd protect her from harm—or anyone who put her in its path.

Trevor stood on the porch looking out over the quiet street. Streetlights illuminated the lawn and he could still hear the sound of children playing in dark yards. Hope walked out of the house and directly behind him. She wrapped her arms around him and rested her cheek on his back.

"Thank you," she whispered.

"For what?" He laid his hands over her hands, which were pressed to his chest.

"For coming." She let her arms slide around him as he turned around to face her. Her eyes lowered from his, and after a moment she looked back up at him. "I'm sorry about Carissa's inquisition."

"She's looking out for you. Your entire family is."

"But I didn't like the way she said things to you."

He brushed the wisps of hair from her forehead. "I'm not worried about it. I'm not sure I passed with flying colors tonight, but as long as you still like me."

"I'm finding I like you an awful lot."

"I really like the sound of that."

"Why don't I go inside and tell Carissa to take my car home. I want you to come home with me." Her were dark, and passion and need stirred in them.

His heart and his body were in a battle. The heart told him to kiss her good night. His body urged him to accept the offer. How could he refuse? He'd been infatuated with her from his dreams. Then the picture of her had haunted him. Now, standing with her in his arms, he was feeling a powerful emotion he'd never felt before.

He held her tight, then made himself step back from her. "No."

"No?" Her brows knit and it was adorable.

"No." He kissed her again, this time on the top of the head. "I won't let you choose me over your father. Not tonight. You owe him a chess game and you owe your sister some idle gossip when I'm out of sight."

Hope blew out a breath and pouted.

He brushed her lips with his thumb. "Promise me I can have a rain check?"

"I promise."

"Good night, Hope." He lowered his lips to hers and softly kissed her. He'd love to take more, but knowing he'd not won any prizes with her family, he didn't want to have any eyes watching from inside decide he was after Hope for the wrong reasons.

She stood in the glow of the house, her arms folded over her chest. He'd never seen anyone so beautiful.

"Hey," he called from the car as he opened his door. "You forgot to tell me where you were when I got here,"

"I finished your painting."

"Already?"

"Inspiration strikes when it feels like it."

"I can't wait to see it. Can I come by in the morning?"

"I kinda hoped you would," she said, placing a kiss on the tips of her fingers and blowing it toward him.

God, he had completely lost his heart. He needed to call Donald Buchanan and end the wait tonight. He couldn't hide things from her anymore.

Chapter Five

Hope walked through the door to the kitchen and watched as her parents passed admiring looks at one another over sudsy water.

David gave her a glance. "Game's all set up. Are you ready?"

"Yep."

"Let's get it started. I don't think Carissa's going to let me keep you too long." He winked and then kissed his wife.

Wrapping his arm around Hope, he walked her toward the chessboard that sat in the corner of the living room. He'd pulled up the two wingback chairs, as usual. Hope sat down across from her father and moved her pawn.

David answered with his pawn and waited for Hope's next move. "Trevor seems like a nice man."

"He is, Dad."

"Looks like you'd like to get to know him better."

"Uh-huh." She moved her knight only to see it whisked away. "Darn!"

"We should play when your head is full of other things more often."

"Bite your tongue." She moved her rook into place and laughed as she took his knight. "Watch your back, old man."

"And I thought you were playing nice since your head was in the clouds." David smiled as he moved another pawn.

"I wanted to ask you a question." She kept her voice low, making sure her voice wouldn't carry to the kitchen.

"What is it?"

"I don't want to hurt your feelings." She rolled the king in her hand, taking it off the board and inevitably ending the game. "I don't want to hurt Mom either."

"Hope, is everything okay?" David reached across the board and laid his hand on hers. His brows had drawn together, leaving worry lines streaked across his forehead.

"Yes. Everything is fine. I didn't mean to scare you."

"Well, you are."

"I'm sorry." She blew out a breath and looked up at him. His chocolate eyes creased with age and wisdom. With a smile she hoped conveyed her love for him, she said, "I want to find out about my birth parents."

He didn't speak or move right away. But when he did, it was fury she saw in his eyes, followed by the hurt she hadn't wanted to cause.

"Why don't we take this conversation out to the front porch." He stood and walked toward the front door.

Hope closed her eyes and took a deep, cleansing breath, but it didn't take away regret she felt from telling him what she'd wanted to do. How could she feel so small?

When she walked out of the house, he was sitting on the porch swing looking out over the dark street. He lifted his head to acknowledge the seat next to him. She knew he expected her to take it.

The deep breath he took and the clearing of his throat said he was ready to discuss what she'd said. Hope braced herself for the calm and grueling argument that loomed before her.

"I thought perhaps this would have been a phase you'd have gone through at thirteen, not twenty-three."

"I don't want you to be disappointed in me."

"Hope Katherine, I'm not." He set his jaw. "If I had wanted to hide your birth mother from you, I would have. There hasn't been a day in your life that you didn't know you were given to us as a gift." He reached to her face and touched her chin with is finger and thumb, as he had when she was a small girl. "I love you. Your mother loves you. As long and you are not going to replace us as your family, I will listen to what you have to say."

"Dad, I would never think of doing that."

"I know," he said, releasing his grip. "It's still going to sting." David took a deep breath, laid his arm across her shoulders, and pulled her into him.

Hope rested her head on his shoulder. It was stiffer than it had been any time before. She was hurting him and she couldn't help it, but he was trying not to show it. Hope nuzzled in even closer to her father and gathered her thoughts. "I know she's dead. I know there isn't a lot of good to her, but Dad, there's another part. Someone else was involved. Curiosity has the better of me. I want to know that other half. I want to know why she couldn't or wouldn't tell him about me." Hope felt him shift away from her the slightest bit. She sat up and looked into his eyes again. "I don't want to replace you. I couldn't have been happier with my life. It's always been perfect. I just want to know whose blood runs through my veins."

He only nodded. She was sure he wanted to stop her. Had he asked her to, she would probably have dropped the whole thing, but he wasn't asking her to drop it. Worse, he wasn't saying anything.

"I love you and Mom. And Carissa and Thomas and the kids are my life."

"Shh." He put his finger to her lips. "Are you ready for it? Are you ready to either have your answers or to be disappointed in what you learn?"

"I think I am."

"It's going to change you, Hope."

"I'm not looking for it to change me."

"What I mean is you'll have so much more information than you do now. Look at how your sister reacts when you even mention Mandy Marlow. Her face loses its color and her lips get tight. What she remembers isn't positive. You are the only thing about Mandy that was ever positive to Carissa. She would have fought me to keep you if she'd had to."

"I know."

"Then take what you know and consider it might get worse. What if the man who fathered you is some drug pusher? What if he's a drunk or a serial killer?"

"What if he's some even-mannered pilot who met a woman?" she asked, and David shook his head.

"You certainly can give as well as you get."

"I'm not replacing you."

"So you've said."

"I just want facts. And I want to be open and honest about this. I don't want to hide it from you."

"I assume Trevor is going to help you do this?"

She nodded, and David took his arm from her shoulders and ran his fingers through his hair.

"He's already given me a file full of information, but I think he has more. I just think he's afraid to show me. I'll find her family myself if I have to."

"You'll what?" The voice came from the front door, and both Hope and David turned their heads toward Sophia.

"Mom…"

"You're contacting her family?"

"Mom…" Hope stood and David followed.

"What are you doing? We've been open and honest with you. You know everything we've ever known about the woman. Why are you trying to build another family?"

"I'm not," she started.

"Hope, why would you want…"

"Sophie." David laid a gentle hand on her shoulder. "She just wants to know who the people were that gave her life."

"We gave her a life," her mother snapped back.

"Not a life, Mom. Life. I don't need a new mother. I don't want another father. I want to know about the people who created me. When I have children I would like to know if they should be screened for certain things or if I might carry some gene for disease."

"Children? Now you're having children?" Sophia clasped her hands to her chest.

"No." Hope shook her head and walked toward her mother. "Yes, someday I'll have children. Right now, I want to know who gave me to you so you could be my mother. Even Santa leaves tags on gifts, Mom. My tag was half torn off." She reached for her mother's hand. "I need to know. I need your blessing."

Sophia looked at David, who silently nodded.

"Please, Mom."

"Fine." She pulled her hand back. "You have my blessing."

Hope's heart felt like it was tearing in two when her mother turned back to the house and walked inside.

"She'll be fine," her father assured her. "I'll talk to her."

"Thank you."

"You'd better talk to your sister. This will affect her."

"She knows."

David nodded. "I'll try and remember everything I can to help you but something tells me Trevor will have more luck."

"I know he will."

"Be careful," he warned. "Don't be afraid to back away if you have to."

"Okay."

"I'd better get in with your mother. I love you."

"I love you too." She stepped forward to hug him, but he'd already walked through the door and disappeared to find his wife and comfort her. Hope fought back the urge to cry. She couldn't give up. She had to know the truth—she only wished it didn't hurt those she loved.

Trevor flew through the door and headed straight for the desk. He might be a slob in the rental car, but his paperwork was immaculate. His fingers tore through the papers until he found Donald Buchanan's phone number. It was time for him to come clean or Trevor would do it for him.

"Hello," a woman's voice answered. Shit!

"I'm sorry, ma'am. I was looking for a Mr. Buchanan. I think I have the wrong—"

"This is his wife. What can I do for you?" The voice was clear and sharp. The image of the grandmother from Flowers in the Attic flashed in his mind. The hair on his arms stood and his skin chilled.

"I'm a business associate. I can call at a later…"

"I said what can I do for you?"

"Nothing, ma'am. I'll call another time. Thank you," he said and disconnected the phone call.

What had he gotten himself into? Donald Buchanan had warned him against letting his wife know what was going on. He'd said he feared for Hope's safety.

If Trevor couldn't stop Donald Buchanan, he had to stop Hope.

"I can't believe you told Dad and upset Mom like that." Carissa's arms flew in the air inside the confines of Hope's car. "Did you see her face? She was heartbroken."

"You would rather I didn't say anything? You would rather I find out my answers behind her back and never tell her?"

"What I'm saying, Hope, is she shouldn't have found out by overhearing it. You should have had them both right there with you when you discussed it. Not starting with Dad and then moving on to Mom."

"I didn't mean to tell him right then. It just came out," she said as she drove down Carissa's street.

"You'd better do this all fast. It's killing Mom that you need to do it at all. I hope that Trevor knows what he's doing."

"That Trevor?" Hope was sure to hear Carissa's opinion on him now. "You know, you weren't very nice to him."

"I don't trust him."

"Why?"

"Why?" Carissa snorted out a laugh. "He picked you up in a cemetery."

"He didn't pick me up." She held back her own laugh and shook her head.

"Either way. He meets you in a cemetery, mourning over someone you shouldn't have been mourning over anyway," she added, living up to Hope's prediction. "Then he comes into the school and inquires about our classes when his niece doesn't even live here? And then...oh and then he happens into your store, and now you're painting his picture."

"I was already painting it," she admitted, wrinkling up her nose. She caught her sister's stare. "I couldn't get his face out of my mind. I've seen it in my dreams. Just like Grandma Katie said, He'll come for you."

"I have decided you've lost your ever-loving mind."

"I haven't, but I might be losing my heart." The smile was there. She felt it on her face and her whole body felt light.

"Oh, dear Lord!" Carissa shoved though the contents of her purse for her keys. "I can't believe you. You need a shrink."

"So now you're going to go to bed mad at me too? Mom's mad. You're mad. Dad's not too happy…"

"And you think going on with this is going to change that? Stop while you're ahead."

"I can't," she said softly. "I need to do this."

"Then be careful with who you hurt with it." Carissa opened the door to the car. "And by the way, I'd really reconsider this Trevor guy too. I swear he's hiding something. I don't know what it is, but—"

"And when you're wrong and I marry the man?" She raised her eyebrows as a dare.

"Then I'll take it all back. But, hell, Hope, don't go run off to Vegas and get married tonight to shut me up. I'm allowed to worry about you. It's been my job since the day Mandy walked into the juice store and told me she was pregnant with my sister." She shut the door and waited until Hope rolled down the window. "I love you. Take care of yourself and I'll be happy."

"I will. I promise."

How could she have hurt everyone she loved? But she had.

Hope tossed and turned and sat up in bed. She pulled her hair over her shoulder and huffed out a breath. Was it worth it? Did it really matter who had been part of who created her?

Yes, it did matter. It had always mattered.

Hope swung her feet to the side of the bed and set them on the floor. She slipped her feet into her slippers and walked to the kitchen. Opening the door to the refrigerator, she pulled out the orange juice and reached for a short glass in the cupboard. She sat down at the table and poured the orange juice into the glass. Then she sat with it in her hands, never taking a drink.

So many things had run through her head since she'd told her father about her plans. The pain in her mother's eyes was enough to make her rethink the whole thing. She was used to Carissa being angry with her. That was normal. Sisters were always at each other for something. But it was what she'd said about Trevor that made her anxious.

Carissa didn't trust him. The thought alone angered Hope, but it shouldn't, and that angered her more. Carissa had always watched out for her and now wouldn't be any different. But there were some things that didn't click when Hope thought about them.

Why was Trevor still in Kansas City? What insurance investigation would possibly take so long? Why did he suddenly pop up at the cemetery, the school, and her store?

She finally drank down the juice. She hated herself for thinking too hard. There wasn't anything she wanted more than for Trevor to have all her answers and to be her answer.

Her morning was shaky and dragged on. She'd had three snippy old ladies in her shop, all of whom took jabs at her art. Thomas had new students, and she wanted to tell them to try a quieter form of expression, but she was sure if she did, he'd hit her upside the head with a drumstick. The pants she'd put on didn't fit quite right, and her hair had gone flat in a matter of moments. Had she not wanted Trevor to walk through the door, she'd lock it.

And then he did.

It was past one thirty. He carried a pizza and a two-liter bottle of soda. When he smiled, he looked a bit shaky too. That didn't help her mood.

"Hi," she managed, but it didn't sound polite.

"Hey. I hope you like pizza," he said, lifting it with a forced smile.

"Who doesn't like pizza?" She walked around the counter, brushed his lips lightly with a kiss, and took the pizza from him.

"My sister."

"What?" She turned her head as she walked toward the back of the store.

"My sister. She doesn't like pizza."

"Really?"

He shrugged. "She worked at a pizza place during high school. Might just be she's tired of it for eternity."

"I can't imagine." Hope opened a cabinet and took out two paper plates. She set them on the table and reached for two coffee mugs from her rack.

"I didn't know what you'd want, so I got cheese." He winced as he said it, and she laughed.

"You can't go wrong with that."

Trevor nodded and reached into the box.

"Wait," she said, stopping him.

"What's wrong?"

"I'm in a real lousy mood. The food can wait a minute." She set down the mugs and closed the lid to the pizza. She walked a step closer to him and wrapped her arms around his neck. "I think we should kiss."

"I thought we did that," he said, holding his hands out to the sides.

"No, that was a peck. A spiteful one at that. Hold me and kiss me."

"My hands have cheese and sauce on them." He grinned.

"Fine. I'll hold. You kiss."

He dipped his head down until their lips were a breath apart. The anticipation of the kiss already lifted her spirits. But when his arms came around her, his hands careful not to touch her clothes, and he pulled her to him tight, the air whooshed out of her. He took possession of her lips. She felt the coarseness of his unshaven skin rub against her face as his tongue sought hers.

Hope pulled herself to him tighter and felt her knees go weak. He nipped at her lip, took her mouth again, and left her completely boneless when he pulled away and rested his forehead on hers.

"Okay," she said, catching her breath. "That's better."

"Dear God, do you know what you do to me?" His words were carried on a breathless whisper as well.

She knew exactly what she did to him. She'd pressed herself extremely close and though she'd meant to lock the door she never had. "We'd better eat that pizza."

"We'd better." He stepped back to let her move away from him. Ripping a piece of paper towel from a roll on the table, he wiped off his hands. "Last night I..." He turned his head. "Oh, wow."

Hope lifted her head up and watched as he was pulled toward his portrait.

"She's going to flip. She's just going to flip!"

"Well, that will be a sight," she joked, but a warmth she'd never felt before washed over her as he admired her work.

"Oh, Hope... there are no words." His voice was awed. He cocked his head as he moved in closer to the canvas. "Thank you."

"I mean it."

"So do I, now say thank you." She waited for him to turn his eyes to her.

"Thank you." His lips were soft, but the smile reached his eyes and bore right into her heart.

"I can't wait to see her face when you give it to her."

Trevor moved to her and gathered her in his arms again. "Thank you," he said and kissed her gently. "Thank you." He kissed her again. "Thank you."

"You back there?" The moment fizzled when she heard her sister's voice call from the front door.

"We're back here having lunch," Hope called out.

"We're?" Carissa asked as she cleared the back wall. Her eyes widened and then narrowed as she looked at Trevor. "Oh."

Trevor gave Carissa a nod. "Hello, Carissa. Nice to see you again."

"Trevor," she said coolly, at which Hope shot her a warning with her eyes. "Nice to see you too." She added a smile and Hope took a breath.

"Want some pizza?" Trevor asked her, opening the lid to the box.

"No, I'm trying really hard to lose all that baby fat." She pointed to Hope. "Don't you even point out how old that baby is now."

"Not a word." Hope ran her fingers over her lips as if to zip them.

"Wow." Carissa moved further into the small room and looked over the painting that Hope had finished the night before. "You will never cease to amaze me. This is wonderful."

Hope exchanged glances with Trevor. "Thank you," she said as the bell on the front door chimed. "Excuse me." She left them alone.

Trevor swallowed hard, trying to dislodge the ball of dread stuck in his throat.

"I have some soda. Can I get you some?"

"No, I'm fine," Carissa said, her voice unthreatening. He took that as a positive sign. "She really did a nice job on your portrait."

"She really did. My mom is going to love it."

Carissa nodded. "She sure is. Your mom is in New York?"

He nodded back to her. More examining the boyfriend of the little sister; he'd known this was coming.

"She tells me she has you helping her find out about Mandy."

If nothing else, she was quick to the point of the tension between them. "Yes. She asked me to find out about her. Hope is interested in finding out who her biological father is."

Carissa walked to the seat that Hope would have occupied had they ever had the chance to start lunch. She sat, rubbed her hands on her skirt, and looked up at him. "I don't want her hurt."

"I know. I have no intention of hurting her." He gripped the back of the vacant chair, hoping to keep his calm as Carissa looked him over. Could she see that he was keeping things from Hope? From all of them?

"Ruth Marlow. Have you already found her?"

"Mandy's mother." He walked around the chair and sat down. The mere fact that Carissa had mentioned Mandy's mother meant she was giving up information whether she'd wanted to or not.

Carissa laced her fingers together and set them in her lap. "I contacted her when I was fifteen." Her voice was shaky. "The woman wasn't too cooperative in helping me build a better picture of my mother. She asked me not to contact her again. As far as she was concerned, Mandy Marlow was dead to her when she walked out the door after begging for money."

Ruth Marlow hadn't been a wealth of information to him either.

She sat quietly for a moment. Her knuckles were white, and Trevor watched her shoulders tighten before she shifted her eyes to him. "That is the one and only time I've ever admitted that I sought out Mandy's family. Please promise me you'll never, ever mention it."

"Not a word," he promised, realizing it was a big moment between him and Carissa. She trusted him, and he wasn't going to disappoint her.

"Thank you." The wavering in her voice filled the small room with the tension of her disapproval over what Hope might discover. "I don't know why she has to do this. It really pisses me off."

"She just feels like it's a piece that's missing in her life." The worst part was that he agreed with Carissa, but he had to support Hope.

"I suppose I understand that, but you're encouraging her?"

He shook his head. "No. As a matter of fact, I told her that she wouldn't be finding out anything good. Things don't usually end well when children go in search of their birth parents." He was speaking the words, but he already knew no matter what kind of picture they painted of Mandy Marlow, Donald Buchanan was waiting in the wings and he would be meeting Hope.

"So you think she should stop?"

He shrugged. "I want her to be happy. If this makes her happy, I want to help her with it." And protect her in the process, he thought.

Carissa leaned back in her chair and considered him. It wasn't comfortable having her dark eyes scan over him as they were. "You really care for her?"

"I really do."

"You just met her."

"But I feel like I've known her for years." He shook his head and moved in closer to her. "This is going to sound crazy, but I've had dreams about her."

Carissa's eyes widened. "Dreams?"

"I told you it seemed silly."

"Not so silly," she said as they heard the chime on the door, and he knew Hope would be back in a moment to join them. "If you really care about her, protect her. I don't know who Mandy became after she left the care of my father, but I can't imagine she was an ideal citizen. But I got Hope. And that was what I wanted. Keep her safe," she finished just as Hope walked through the door.

"Eighty-five dollars later," she said, smiling radiantly.

"Good for you." Carissa stood. "I have group lessons in fifteen minutes. I'd better get back. Trevor, it was nice to see you."

"Likewise."

"And you, I'll see you tomorrow." She kissed her sister on the cheek and left through the store.

"Are you finally bonding?" Hope took her seat and pulled a slice of pizza out of the box.

"I suppose you could call it that." He poured soda in her cup, sat back, and watched as she ate. "She doesn't want you hurt by looking into your birth parents."

"Don't care," she said taking another bite. "I'm into it already. If you stop helping me, I'll keep digging on my own."

He kept his eyes on her as she angrily attacked the piece of pizza. He realized he was in a unique position. Because

Mandy had died and Trevor hadn't yet shown a photo of Hope to her birth father, he was the only person in the world who could look at Hope Kendal and see both Donald Buchanan and Mandy Marlow in her. There were certain features that each contributed. How either of them could have made a creature as beautiful as Hope, he'd never know. What she lacked was Mandy's hardness and Donald's directness. What she had was Sophia's kindness and David's patience. No one but him could look at her and know about the Buchanan-Marlow connection. To the world she was a Kendal through and though.

Hope shifted her attention from her pizza to him. With her mouth full she asked, "What's wrong?"

"Not a thing."

"You're staring at me."

"I do that a lot." He laid his hand on her knee. "Hope, I'm not going to stop helping you look for your answers. I'll use it as an excuse to keep seeing you every day if I have to."

Hope set down the pizza, took a sip of her drink, and moved in closer to him. "You don't need an excuse to see me every day. I would be heartbroken now if I didn't see you every day."

"I never believed in love at first sight," he said inching closer to her. "When I first laid eyes on you I was a goner."

"Last night you said something about maybe settling down in Kansas City. Did you mean that? Would you really relocate here?"

"Do you have cars here?"

"Yes."

"Do you have houses?"

"Yes."

"Jewelry, ex-husbands, boats, and farms?"

She laughed, her eyes still locked on his. "Yes, what does that all mean?"

"It means that I could still work here. In my field, that's all I need."

Hope let her shoulders drop and her head tilted to the side. "I can't believe you walked into my life."

He couldn't believe it either. Now he just had to keep working on earning and keeping her trust so that when she learned the truth about his work for Buchanan she wouldn't turn around and walk out of his life.

They'd gone to dinner and went back to her place. They'd rented a movie, but they never saw any of it. They'd sat on the couch and made out like a couple of fifteen-year-olds. He chuckled to himself. That had been great.

It had taken everything he had to walk out and go back to his hotel, but he'd done it. She might have gone to bed cursing him, but in the end, he'd be a hero for it. At least that's what he kept telling himself, since he wanted to tangle himself in her sheets, wrapped in her arms at that very moment.

Trevor pulled a beer from the mini fridge in the corner and twisted off the cap. He'd have to decide what course he was going to take, as he couldn't live in a hotel indefinitely. Smiling to himself, he pulled his cell phone from his pocket and called his mother. If anyone could help him make his decision, it was his mother.

Violet Jacobs filled her son's ear with new accounts she'd landed, her recent tennis match wins, and of course, a barrage of questions about the case he was working on. But when he filled her in on Hope her underlying tone was one of happiness. He didn't have to tell her he was thinking of relocating to Kansas City; she announced it while he was still drawing the breath to say it himself. Just as she accepted that Hope was the woman of his dreams, and she understood his heart was quickly being lost to her, she knew he had to move on.

His next call would need to be to his roommate.

"Jesus, Trev, you said you'd be back in three days. Where the hell are you?"

"I'm still in Kansas City."

"Sorry to hear they don't have phones!" He was yelling into the phone and that had Trevor laughing. "You know that redhead on the fourth floor has been asking about you."

"Really." He grinned. "Well, maybe you'd better console her for me."

"Damn!" He heard the sigh on the other end of the line. "You frickin' fell in love while you were there."

"I didn't say that," he said on a laugh.

"Didn't have to. I've known you since we were what, eleven? You don't turn down a redhead with legs to her ass and a stack like that, unless you gave up on all other women. That's just what you've done, huh?"

Trevor pulled from his beer and thought about the way even thinking about Hope made his heart beat harder. Yeah, that's what he'd done.

"I have a special person here."

"Special person, my ass. God, did you give her a damn ring or something?"

"If I did?"

"Oh, shit!"

"No." He was laughing now. "I didn't give her a ring."

"Hell, you're thinking about it. Dammit! What the hell am I going to do?"

Trevor laughed again. That was Bryce tried and true. Instead of finding the good in Trevor finding love, he'd decided something bad was going to happen for him.

"Maybe you should see if the redhead wants to room with you. Split the rent. Maybe you could make my room an office."

"Your room an office? Where would she sleep?" Trevor didn't answer right away. "Oh... oh! I get it," Bryce finally answered and laughed. "Yeah, that would be nice."

"I'll be home in two weeks for my mom's birthday. I'll bring my woman to see you."

"Yeah, you'd better."

"Then we can talk about the apartment."

"Shit! You're moving out."

"Yeah, I guess I am." He smiled to himself realizing he'd better start looking for his own place.

"Well I guess it's time. I knew you wouldn't want to bachelor with me forever."

"Sorry, friend. Hey, I'll call you and let you know what the definite plans are for our visit."

"Sure you will. Just like you said you'd be home in three days."

"Love ya, man."

"Yeah, screw you."

Trevor made almost every phone call he figured he should, except for one. It was past midnight so the call to Donald Buchanan would have to wait until the morning. He'd also need to get to work on figuring out how he was going to lead Hope to her answers.

God, how much deeper in could he get?

Chapter Six

Hope secured the canvas into the frame she had chosen for Trevor's portrait. She spread a protective cloth on the table so she could turn the painting over and finish the back.

Tuesday mornings were among her busiest times. Thomas and Carissa hosted new parents meetings, and afterward those parents would wander into her shop and spend their money. That was exactly what had happened that morning, which had given her day a fabulous start.

As she finished the back of the of the frame, her cell phone rang in her pocket.

"Hello."

"Hello, beautiful."

"Ah, the voice I was just thinking of," she said as she turned over the painting and examined it. His dark eyes looked up at her. "What are you up to, handsome?"

"Making phone calls. Printing out paperwork. Looking for an apartment."

She put down the frame.

"Trevor, did you just say you were looking for an apartment?"

"Yeah," he said, his voice light. "Sounds like my roommate is going to put the moves on the redhead upstairs."

"Oh. I thought..." She let it go. She didn't want to think about him moving back to New York, even if it was inevitable.

"Yeah, what did you think?"

"I guess I thought you were going to move here."

"I am."

Her breath caught in her lungs. "Really?"

"Hope, I want to be here. I'd really like to see if things could work out between us. Don't you?"

"Yes, of course. I just... well, I was just ready..." She blew out a ragged breath. "I just was so prepared for you to go back. I want you here."

"Good. I'm going to get in a full day of work, call a client, and see a few places. Then when you get off work, I'm coming over."

"Trevor." She raised her hand to her chest and felt the rapid beat of her heart. "Bring a bag. You're not going home tonight."

He was silent for a moment. "You've just committed to that, you know."

"I committed to it the first time I asked you to stay with me. This time I'm just holding you to it."

When she hung up the phone, she held her hand to her stomach. Flutters of anticipation and fear stirred inside her. The anticipation was overwhelming. Was she woman enough to keep him forever?

Trevor sat in his hotel surrounded by piles of papers all with Mandy Marlow's name on them. He searched each of them trying to pull together another package to give to Hope. This time he decided he wanted to try and piece something together that would give her a little hope that the blood that ran through her wasn't completely bad.

Guilt weighed him down. The first set of papers he'd given her he'd done his best to paint the ugliest picture so she'd drop the idea of searching. It hadn't worked, and he wasn't finding much to help his new cause of building Mandy into a nicer person.

Still, he wanted to get in touch with Donald Buchanan and move things forward. He'd had Hope Kendal in his grasp for over a week and the man had paid him to get close to her. Though he hadn't needed Donald's money to get closer to her. He'd gone and fallen completely in love with her on his own.

What didn't make sense was why Donald Buchanan hadn't come forward to meet Hope. This was what he'd wanted, after all. It wasn't as if Trevor had approached him on the subject. No, Donald Buchanan had walked into his office on that fine July morning, laid down the money to have his lover found, and find the truth behind a child he assumed he had.

Trevor picked up the phone and dialed the cell number Buchanan had given him.

"Hello." Again, the crisp voice on the other end was a woman.

Trevor looked down at the number on the piece of paper in his hand. He'd been instructed not to call the office or his home, so the woman's voice came as a surprise. "I am looking for Donald Buchanan."

"He's not available."

"Do you know when he will be available?"

"There is no need for you to call back," she said, and the line went dead.

Something wasn't playing out right. Donald Buchanan had disappeared in the past few days. Trevor could only assume the hard-assed woman who answered the phone was his wife. He shook his head. Why had Donald warned him about her and then disappeared?

A knot tightened in the pit of his stomach. If Donald Buchanan didn't come forward before he and Hope made their trip to New York for his mother's birthday, he'd come clean with what he knew. He'd protect his client, but Hope was his client too. Above being his client she was the woman he wanted to spend the rest of his life with. He wanted to insure that was going to be a long and prosperous one for both of them.

"Clock is ticking, Buchanan. Either you come out of hiding or you miss your opportunity to meet your daughter."

He didn't want Hope to think he was planning to take advantage of her when he showed up at her house with a haircut, new shirt, cologne splashed on, a duffle bag full of clothes, and his toothbrush. He'd picked up a dozen roses, in a vase, so he didn't seem cheap.

He'd have brought her a bottle of wine too, but his hands were full.

Trevor rang the doorbell, hid behind the arrangement, and waited for the woman he adored to answer.

He waited and waited. Finally, he looked around the arrangement to make sure he had the right apartment number.

"You know, handsome, you're as good looking from the back as you are from the front."

Trevor turned to see her standing on the walk looking up at him.

"How long have you been there?"

"Long enough to enjoy the view." She walked toward him with her arms full of groceries. "Thought I'd better get enough food for breakfast since I'm keeping you and not letting you go tonight."

She nipped his lip with a kiss.

"Are you still sure you want to do that?"

"When I open this door and put this bag down, I'll explain why I'm not worried about quick romances."

She unlocked the door and pushed it open so they could both walk through.

Trevor closed it behind them and followed her into the kitchen. She set the bags down on the counter and turned to him.

"These are for you." He held out the vase.

"That is the most beautiful arrangement I've ever seen."

"I thought it reflected its recipient."

"Thank you," she said as she set it in the middle of the table. "You look nervous."

"Why? I shouldn't be. I've already met the man who will kick my ass if I hurt his daughter. Having an intimate evening with her shouldn't make me nervous."

She moved in closer again and brushed his lip with hers. "I guess he'll have to get used to the thought."

Trevor could only nod.

"But right now I'm hungry. So I'm going to make you a meal you'll never forget. One that will have you wanting to marry me and never leave." She laughed, but he couldn't.

"I don't need a meal to know that already," he said, his voice steady and sure.

Her eyes opened wide and she let out a breath. "Trevor, I was kidding. I'm not working on making you marry me."

He nodded. Maybe she didn't feel the same way he did. He definitely was going to find out, but for tonight, he was going to enjoy a meal and the company of a beautiful woman.

Hope went about putting away the groceries. "Why don't you open the wine I have chilling in the fridge. Glasses are…"

"Right over here," he said reaching around her, brushing his body against hers, and pulling the glasses from the cupboard before turning and setting them on the table.

"I forgot. You've dined here before."

"Corkscrew?" he asked as he pulled the wine from the refrigerator.

"Drawer next to you." She pointed and he turned to open the drawer.

"So what are you making to seduce me?"

"Please tell me you like scallops."

"I like scallops."

"Spinach salad?"

"Sounds good so far." He poured wine into each glass and handed her one. "You have more. Continue." He moved closer to her until she'd backed against the counter.

"Um, asparagus and for dessert baked pears."

He backed up and looked down into her deep blue eyes. "Pears?"

"You don't like pears?"

He shrugged. "Pears yes. Baked pears, never tried them."

A sexy smile slid across her mouth and she raised her glass to her lips. "I think you'll enjoy them."

"I think it will only be the start of dessert," he said as he moved into her and kissed her hard on the mouth.

He felt her body go soft against his. Her arm encircled his neck and her mouth opened to his. There was a chance he'd misread her. Perhaps she did want all the things he was already sure he wanted.

When he eased back, she stood before him a satisfied look on her face, her eyes still closed. Her sexy smile told him she was ready for him to touch her more, taste her more, and to give her everything he had to offer.

They ate and drank wine while they made small talk over dinner. He told her about growing up in New York and she reciprocated with stories of a quiet life in Kansas City under the watchful eye of her mother and older sister.

After dessert Trevor leaned back in his chair and patted his stomach. "Well, I now know I like baked pears."

"I'm glad to hear it."

"Where did you learn to cook?"

"My mother mostly. Once I was born, she stopped touring and took on a lot of different rolls. She was a teacher at Carissa's school. Room mother in my classrooms. She took care of my great-grandma Katie and"—she motioned to the plates—"she perfected cooking."

"She sounds well rounded."

"Yes she does," she said lifting her wine glass to her lips.

"Did she ever miss touring?"

"Oh I don't think so. She wanted nothing more than to be a mother and that's what she was—a full time, completely attentive mother." She smiled again, but he noticed it vanished quickly and her brows knit.

"There's something about your mother, something that's bothering you." He slid his hand across the table and covered hers.

"She found out about me asking you for help in finding out about Mandy and my birthfather."

Trevor adjusted in his chair. "Found out? You didn't tell her?"

Hope shook her head. "No. I was telling my father and she overheard. I was going to tell her. Honestly I was. But it just happened." She let out a breath. "I broke her heart."

"So you're giving up? You don't want to pursue this?"

"No. I'm not giving up."

That wasn't what he'd wanted to hear, but he let her continue.

"I want it over as quickly as possible."

He could feel the evening taking a drastic turn. On one hand he could end it right there. He could tell her about Donald Buchanan and it would all be over. Then again, it wasn't how it worked. He'd been asked to wait. He would wait.

Hope reached for his hand and ran her thumb gently over his knuckles. "What can I do to help out? What would you usually ask a client if they were looking for someone?"

"Well," he considered. "I'd ask about name, place of birth, last time they were seen." He sipped his wine and set the glass back down. "Then I'd ask if they had anything that belonged to the person."

"Like personal belongings?"

"Yeah, anything is helpful."

"Like a purse? Or at least items that would have been in someone's purse."

"I suppose that would do." He looked her over as she chewed on her lip. "Do you have something that personally belonged to Mandy?"

Hope sat quietly for a moment then rose from the table. She returned with a box and set it on the table. "This is all that was left," she said. "She sold everything she had before she found my dad and Carissa. She didn't want there to be anything left." She shrugged.

"May I?"

"Of course." She pushed the box closer to him.

He opened it and looked inside. As Hope had said, the box was filled with what would have been, he assumed, the contents of Mandy's purse and the final documents that closed out her existence. He lifted her wallet and opened it.

"There are still thirty dollars in here."

She shrugged again. "It wasn't mine to take."

A warmth filled him. Only someone as sweet as Hope would still consider that someone else's. He looked at her driver's license and pulled it from the windowed pocket in the wallet. "Your dad never married her but she had his last name?"

Hope nodded. "He said she changed it so that it would match his. It made everything easier when I was born. They had the same last name. No questions were asked."

"You don't keep her death certificate in a safer place than this?" He pulled it from the box.

"It's just a copy."

Trevor replaced the certificate. "These are her keys?" he asked as he pulled them from the box.

"Yes. I don't know what they went to. Dad said she had a car and they sold it to cover her burial. But she didn't have a house or anything else. She was staying in some motel before I was born."

He lifted each of the four keys on the ring and then he stopped.

"Do you know what this is?" He held up one of the keys on the ring.

Hope shook her head.

"It's a safety deposit box key."

"Why would she have a key to a safety deposit box?"

"Why not?" He lifted everything out of the box and laid it out on the table.

Hope picked up the dishes and carried them to the sink to make more room, then sat back down.

"None of this paperwork has anything to do with a bank account," he said.

"Don't you think my father would have looked into that?"

Trevor nodded. "Yeah, he seems like a pretty thorough man."

"He is," she said warmly.

Trevor went through the wallet again and this time pulled out each item. He looked at every business card, her driver's license, and credit cards. Nothing out of the ordinary. He sat back in his seat.

They didn't speak. She was letting him process the information he had just acquired. He didn't tell her the information he had in his own mind, but it wouldn't have mattered. There wasn't much that was new... except the key.

He ran his fingers through each of the slots. He started in the change compartment and then the bill compartment. He checked the credit card slots, one by one. The wallet was empty. Only then did he notice a small hole in the coin area. He pulled it back slightly and grinned.

Hope's eyes opened wide. "What is it?"

"Probably nothing," he said as he pulled out a thin shred of paper with a number written on it. "It could be a phone number."

He handed the paper to her and she looked at it. "It doesn't have a KC area code."

"Where was she born?" he asked even though he had the answer to that.

"New York."

"Doesn't match any New York area codes either." He looked it over and then lifted his eyes to her. He picked up the keys. "Hope, do you think this is the account number to the safe-deposit box?"

Her eyes grew wider. "I don't know. How would we find out?"

"This is when I do my job. Can I take these?"

"Of course. What are you going to do?"

"We're going to start by mapping out the area around where you were born. "Do you know which motel she was staying in?"

"No."

"Do you think you could find out?" He tilted his head and he knew she understood his thought.

She blew out a breath and knit her brows. "Yeah, I suppose I could ask."

Trevor moved toward her and kissed her on the lips gently. "At this point it can't hurt, right?"

"Right," she said uneasily.

"In the meantime, this is what I'll do. I'll pinpoint the motels in the area nearest your parents' house. She would have wanted to be close to your father and the hospital. So chances are she was somewhere in between. Then we'll do a map of the banks in the radius that were open twenty-three years ago." He smiled. He loved that there was something new to a case that he'd thought he had all the information to. "Then you'll have to step up and do some calling. Your father has the power of attorney, I assume?"

"I would think so."

"We may have to work with him for you to get it."

"I don't like involving them."

"Hope, why would she have the box? She needed something kept safe. You are the rightful owner of whatever it is."

He watched her process what he'd said. She filled her wine glass, chewed her lip, and finally stood and leaned against the cabinet.

"I don't want to hurt them."

"I know."

"What do I do?"

Trevor stood and walked to her. He placed his hands on her waist and pulled her close to him. "Walk away, then."

"I can't."

"Then you have to ask." He raised his brows to her and she sighed.

"You're right. Okay. I'll ask."

"Now." He took her wine glass and set it to the side. "As much as I adore talking business with a client, I'm sure this wasn't what you'd planned to do tonight."

Hope lifted her arms around his neck and pulled his mouth down to hers. "You're right."

She consumed his mouth with hers. Her hands moved down to his chest and she began unbuttoning his shirt. She slid her hands inside the fabric and his heart kicked up a notch when her hands touched his skin.

He was going to lose control. He felt it. He wanted it.

He pulled her legs up around his waist, his mouth hot and persistent on hers. Maneuvering through her apartment, he walked into the living room.

"I'm at a loss," he managed between breaths when he noticed there were several doorways. "Where is your bedroom?"

"Down the hall. On the right."

He started down the hallway and found the door to her room. He carefully moved through the room lit only by moonlight filtering through the window.

Finally, he hit the bed with his shins. "Crap!"

"Are you hurt?" She laughed and held him tighter.

"No." He crushed his mouth back to hers as he lowered her to the bed beneath him.

With her hands wandering over his chest, he moved his body atop hers. He'd dreamed of that very moment so many times. She felt so right underneath him.

"Trevor, I've dreamed of you doing this to me," she said, and he pulled back to look down at her in the shadows.

"What?"

"I've dreamed of you making love to me. I've seen your face for years."

His mouth went dry. Was it possible for two people to find each other under such crazy circumstances?

"I've waited for you," she said, pulling him down against her, pushing his shirt from his shoulders.

His hands roved between them until he managed the button on her pants, then he slid them from her hips and they landed on the floor. Placing soft kisses down her neck, he pulled her shirt over her head with only a brief interruption of his lips on her skin. Her chest rose and fell beneath his touch and when he removed her bra and filled his hands with her, she let loose a moan that ignited his core.

Hope pushed at his pants until they fell to the floor with hers. Finally, they lay skin to skin. He wanted to touch her, taste her, fill his senses with her. He wanted to take it slow, but he'd waited so long for the moment, he wasn't sure he could.

Common sense pushed its way through as Hope ran her hands down his back.

"Hold on," he whispered.

"What's wrong?"

"The condom is in my wallet. On the floor."

"I bought some," she whispered, and he moved back to her mouth. "They're on my nightstand."

Her breath was uneasy. "I hope they're the right ones."

He had to stop. "Why would you say that?"

"I've never bought them before."

"I would have taken care of that, Hope."

She shivered beneath him. The moonlight illuminated her, and he could see there was more than just a chill in the room or the anticipation of making love with him for the first time that caused worry to cross her face. "Hope, what's wrong?"

"Nothing. Nothing is wrong. I want this so much."

"You're shaking."

"I've been waiting for you my whole life."

He slid to the side of her, his body protesting, but his heart needed to listen before he went further.

"What do you mean?"

He felt her swallow hard and watched as she collected her thoughts. "I've had dreams about you. My grandmother said you'd come for me. I've waited. I've waited for you."

Suddenly the room did grow colder and he began to shake. He closed his eyes and accepted the surreal moment. They'd dreamed of each other. She'd waited for him because her grandmother had told her he would come. Premonition? Fate? It was a lot to swallow when his body wanted to take and his heart wanted to accept. "Hope," he said, opening his eyes and looking down at her. "You've been waiting for me? You've never made love to anyone else?" He watched as she shook her head from side to side. "Oh, God!"

Trevor sat up and scrubbed his hands over his face. He didn't remember feeling this much pressure in the backseat of Mary Jo Roberts's car when he was fifteen and she was seventeen. He seemed to have handled it just fine then.

"Trevor, please don't stop."

"Hope, how can you say you waited for me for this? You've known me just over a week."

"I've been waiting for you. You have to trust me when I say that."

He did. He knew exactly what it was like to dream up the woman you loved. The proof was Hope Kendal lying next to him naked ready to give up her virtue to him.

"Maybe we should wait."

"I've waited long enough." She pulled him down toward her. "I want to make love to you, tonight. Please, Trevor. Love me. Make love to me."

Her hands ran down his arms and over his back as her mouth lifted to his. How could he say no? He couldn't. His body and his heart wouldn't allow it.

A moment later, he was moving atop her, rolling on the condom, ready to take from her what she'd held on to longer than any other woman he'd known.

Reminding himself to go slow and take it easy, he watched her eyes. They remained locked on his, filled with heat and passion. Her hands urged him on until he pushed himself, slowly, inside of her.

Her body trembled beneath his, but her hands held him tight against her. She moved against him, creating a rhythm. The heat between their bodies began to rise. Hope threw back her head, exposing her neck. He pressed his lips to the hammering pulse at her throat as he moved with her. Her moans vibrated against his lips, and as he climbed toward that peak, he could feel her close in tight around him.

Her lips quivered against his. Her fingernails clawed at his flesh. Her voice carried his name as he took her to that edge and spilled over with her.

After, he held her close. Their hearts raced at the same pace. She'd given herself to him body and heart. How could he ever let go?

Together they lay in the same spot, their legs intertwined, their arms draped over one another. Their hearts still beating the same rhythm.

"I'm going to want to do that a lot more." He smiled down at her.

"I'm glad I waited for you." Her lashes fluttered up as she spoke, and the soft smile of her lips tugged at him.

"I've never felt anything like that. It's like that first time we touched. That same electricity between us." She gave him the slightest nod and he knew she'd felt it. There would never be anyone else again. He knew that.

The sun filled the room with warmth as it filtered in through the curtains. Hope breathed him in, afraid to move, afraid to wake him. She'd never awoken in a bed with a man and she realized she never wanted to wake in one again without him.

Trevor stirred, his eyes opening slowly. A smile slid across his lips and her heart began to race at the mere thought that he was happy to be there still wrapped in her arms.

"Good morning," he said softly.

"Good morning," she returned, but her voice shook.

He lifted his head and propped himself up on his elbow. "Everything okay?" he asked as he traced his finger over her jaw.

"I've never woken with anyone before. I'm afraid to leave this bed."

"I was thinking last night that I don't ever want to wake in a bed with another person but you again."

"Really?"

He nodded. "Do you believe in fate?"

"Fate? Yeah," she said on a sigh. "I believe in fate."

"I believe it was fate that sent me to you. And I know we haven't physically known each other for too long, but in my soul I've known you for a very long time."

"My grandmother has always come to me in my dreams," she said shifting so that she faced him and propped herself up on her elbow as he was. His arm lay lazily over her hip and his fingers drew small circles on her skin. "She told me you would come."

He smiled. "She did, huh?"

"Don't laugh. But yeah, she told me you'd come looking for me."

His dark lashes fluttered as he smiled before he moved in and gently kissed her. "What else did she say?"

"Your touch would be intense and I would fall in love with you."

"I'd say our touches were intense," he said, running his hand down her arm.

"And I'd say I've fallen in love with you."

His brows knit. The slightest fear crept into her.

"Hope, don't say things like that unless you mean them."

"I wouldn't have said it if I didn't mean it. I have fallen in love with you."

The fear left her when he smiled, and the smile was knowing and loving. "Hope, your grandmother never came to me and said I'd fall in love with you. But I believe in fate." He took a deep breath. "About two years ago I began to have dreams. I had dreams about this fair-skinned, blue-eyed blonde," he said, tunneling his fingers though her hair. "And the moment I saw you, I knew it was you. I knew I'd been steered in your direction."

"Really?" Her voice was light.

"Yes." He moved so that she was on her back and he looked down on her. "Hope, I was in love with you before I met you. Now that I have you wrapped in my arms, I never want to wake without you. I love you."

Tears wanted to break through, but she fought them. He pressed his lips to hers and moved on top of her, making love to her again in the sunlight of a new day.

Much later, Hope moved about her kitchen. A smile permeated her lips as she looked out the window over the sink. She sipped at her coffee, listening to the sounds of another person in her apartment getting ready for the day.

The scent of shaving cream lingered in the air. It felt comfortable having Trevor near.

"Good morning, sweetheart," he said as he moved up behind her, wrapping his arms around her.

"Good morning." She turned her head and kissed him softly. "Trevor, I could get used to this."

"Good. Do you have to go in today?"

"Yes. What about you?" She raised her eyebrows.

"I'm calling banks."

"Then I guess you're working too. I suppose you could make those calls from my shop."

A fleeting shadow darkened his eyes, so fast she might have imagined it. Then he kissed the top of her head. "Now, that would be a benefit, wouldn't it? You do your job, I do mine, and I can kiss you in between."

They eased into the morning of work. Trevor had set himself up at the table in the back room and began plotting out banks in the area and checking them off the list. He kept his files in the trunk of the car to keep Hope from finding them.

On Wednesdays, Hope spent most of the day ordering supplies and placing orders for new items for her shop. She did her bookwork and she'd mentioned to Trevor that she was glad she only had one slow day a week.

Likewise, Thomas and Carissa's school was quiet. Hope told him they saved Wednesday mornings for helping at the kids' school. Their own students wouldn't arrive until the afternoon.

So, the atmosphere was quiet.

Trevor dove into his work. He'd found five banks in a two-mile radius of David and Sophia's home. There were another sixty-seven lying within a thirty-mile radius. Once he had his list, he began to whittle it down by the year that the bank location opened. Twenty-three years was a long time for a bank location to stay open. The list shrank, but not by much.

He walked out of the back room, moving his neck from side to side to work the kink from it.

"We only have twenty-seven phone calls to make."

Hope blew out a breath and scowled. "Bring me the list."

Trevor smiled. "How about something to eat first?"

"Taken care of. My mother is bringing us lunch."

Though he tried, he couldn't help the surprise he knew crept over his face. Trevor walked to her side and gathered her hands in his, kissing the tips of her fingers. "Does she know what we're doing?"

"No, and we aren't going to tell her either."

Trevor nodded. He didn't like getting involved with someone and keeping secrets from her parents, though this time it seemed necessary.

"Maybe I should pick up my papers and put them in my car until she leaves."

Hope considered it. "Maybe you're right."

Trevor kissed her on the cheek and retreated back to the back room to gather his paperwork and laptop.

As he closed the trunk to his car, Sophia pulled up in front of Hope's store. Trevor put on his happy face and tried his best to calm his nerves.

"Hello, Sophia." He crossed the street as she climbed from her car.

"Hello, Trevor. Did you just get here?"

"No. I came in with Hope. I'm using her back room as an office for the day. Just trying to catch up on some paperwork."

Sophia opened the door to the passenger side of the car and pulled out a basket. Trevor walked up behind her.

"Let me help you."

"Thank you," she said handing him the basket and gathering another bag. "I'll bet she loves the company."

"Well, I don't think I've been too social. I've been making phone calls and she's been doing her ordering all day." He opened the door to the store for her. "In fact, I don't think we talked for three hours."

They laughed easily as they walked through the store.

Hope was in the back room adding a folding chair to her small table. When her mother walked through the door, she kissed her on the cheek and took the bag from her hand.

"You went all out, didn't you?" she asked, peeking at what her mother had packed.

"Your father is meeting us here, and Carissa and Thomas were going to go into the school early so they're dropping by too."

Trevor swallowed hard. After the morning of trying to discover the secrets of Hope's other parents, he wasn't sure a full family reunion in a crowded room was what he wanted. Unease filled him. Would they all know what he was doing?

"Hope tells me she finished the portrait of you for your mother," Sophia said as she began to unload loaves of French bread from the bags and assorted meats from the basket she'd packed.

"Yes. Her birthday is at the end of August. I can't wait to see her face," he said, and his gaze shifted toward Hope's.

"I hope she likes it. I'm kinda nervous about giving it to her."

"Why?" Sophia looked up at Hope. "You are an amazing artist. I can't imagine why you would be nervous."

"Because his mother knows his face pretty well. What if she looks at it and thinks it's all wrong?"

"What if she looks at it and sees it through your eyes and realizes she's missed something all along." Sophia smiled, and Trevor's nerves settled. "Trevor, I think she'll love it."

"I know she will."

The chime over the door rang and David called back to them, "I'm here to buy the whole place."

Hope laughed as she moved past them to embrace her father in an enormous hug. He kept one arm around her as he looked at the food his wife set out on the table.

"You did say come by for a sandwich, right?"

"I did." Sophia turned and kissed him. "I think I covered everyone's favorites right down to a small jar of peanut butter and jelly for my grandbabies."

"And to think, you almost gave all of this domestic stuff up to travel Europe."

Trevor watched as her eyes changed. She turned toward David, placed a hand on his cheek, and smiled. "I'm still trying to make up for those years I lost." She placed a gentle kiss on his lips again and Trevor thought he could feel tears tugging at him. He turned and pulled out items from the basket. The sentimental moment he'd just witnessed between two people who loved each other so much made him long for that same connection. In twenty years, would he and Hope share moments like that?

He lifted his eyes to see her. She was smiling at her parents as though she'd appreciated the moment as much as they had.

The ringing of his cell phone interrupted his observation. He reached into his pocket and answered.

"Trevor Jacobs," he said as he walked past Hope and her parents to take the call. "When?"

Hope had walked out of the room and toward him as he spoke. He held up a hand to tell her it was urgent. "I see. And the police?" he asked, and he saw her eyes widen. "Okay. I'll be right there."

"God, Trevor, what happened?" She reached out and touched his arm.

"Someone broke into my hotel room," he whispered, not wanting to alarm her parents, who were probably listening closely whether they meant to or not.

"Oh, God!" She covered her mouth. "Why? What were they looking for?"

He gently pulled Hope through the store toward the front door.

"I don't know." He knew they wouldn't have found anything but his clothing and toiletries. All his files were in the trunk of his car—he didn't want Hope finding them yet either. "I have to go."

"I'll go with you."

"No." He shook his head. "You're not going with me." He gathered her hands in his. They were shaking. "I want you to stay here. You're going to have to tell your parents and your sister because I don't want you to be alone."

She nodded at his instruction. "Why do you think someone did this? Do you think this has to do with Mandy?"

"I don't know. But if it wasn't random and they were looking for something that I have, then maybe they know I've been with you." He kissed her gently. "Don't go back to your place and do not leave this store without someone with you. Tell them what you must, but I want you safe."

She nodded again and gave him a quick, hard kiss on the mouth. "Be careful."

Chapter Seven

Whoever had broken in to Trevor's room had trashed the place, torn down the drapes, turned over the bed. The items Trevor had left were in a pile on the floor.

"Do you have an idea of anyone who would have done this to you?" the police officer asked as he jotted down notes about the room.

"I'm a private investigator. I suppose I could have enemies."

"Anyone tied to a case you might be working on?"

Trevor knew it was tied to the case he was working on, but he wasn't about to tell the officer that. He'd pay for the damage to the room. What he couldn't pay for was any harm that may come to Hope if he spoke.

He shook his head. "It's never happened before."

As he walked farther into the room, his cell phone rang. It was Bryce, and Trevor sure as hell wasn't in the mood to hear about the redhead from upstairs, but to keep the police officer's stare off him he turned his back and took the call.

"Hey, Bryce. What's new?"

"Shit! Shit! Shit!" The string of curses from Bryce had Trevor smiling.

"Redhead break your heart?"

"Asshole, they broke into the apartment!"

Trevor was glad he had his back turned to the officer because he couldn't have hidden the shock that must be plastered across his face.

"Hey, let me call you back in a few."

"What? Can't you hear me, dammit?"

"I heard you. Give me ten," he said, hanging up the phone and turning back to the officer. "Sorry, broken-hearted friend."

The officer nodded. "Well I'll head back to the station and fill this out. We'll be looking into the surveillance tapes for the floor as well. If you come up with anything, please let us know. And drop by the station later today. There'll be an incident report for you to sign."

"Absolutely."

He walked through the room only partially aware that the manager of the hotel and the officer were outside the door. He picked through his clothes. There was nothing ripped or torn. They had only thrown them on the floor. He began to fold them up and dig through the remains of the room to find his suitcase.

"Mr. Jacobs, I apologize for all of this." The hotel manager waved his arms to signal the destruction of the room.

"Please, I know this isn't your fault."

"Well, it appears to be a problem with our cleaning staff, sir. I have reviewed the tapes. The only person who was in your room today was the housekeeper, and we cannot find her."

Trevor nodded. "And my room was the only one destroyed?"

"Yes. It seems she opened the door with the cart parked outside of it. She came back out, shut the door, and walked down the hall to the room where we keep the supplies and left the cart." He shrugged.

Trevor nodded again. This had nothing to do with the housekeeper and he knew it. "Well, nothing is missing and nothing looks broken on my end."

"We would like to offer you another room. On the hotel, of course, for your inconvenience."

"I appreciate that, sir. But I just received a phone call from New York," he said, still holding his cell phone in his hand. "It looks like I'm needed back. I guess my stay was almost over anyway."

"I know the police are investigating this, but if we find anything we will certainly be in touch."

"That would be wonderful."

"I hope you'd consider staying here again," the manager pleaded.

Trevor smiled and shook the man's hand. "My stay was pleasant. This was random. I wouldn't hold it against the hotel."

The manager looked satisfied with that and moved toward the door where Trevor now noticed a security guard posted.

He finished packing his bag and signed all necessary papers with the hotel. He threw his bag into the trunk of his car and headed to the police station to sign some papers there as well.

Trevor made the phone call to Bryce as he left the police station. He'd made him wait three hours and he knew Bryce wasn't going to be happy.

"Bryce." He held the phone away from his ear as the string of curses flew from his roommate.

"They broke into the office too. What the hell are you into? Dammit, you should see this place. They broke all my fucking CDs." He could hear Bryce kicking around items at his feet.

"What did they do to the office?"

"I don't know. Call your mommy. She's the one who found out about the office. I'm stuck here in the shit-hole apartment waiting for the damn cops."

"I'm sorry."

"Ass, you'd better be. Freaked the redhead out. She won't move in now."

He laughed. "Sorry for that too."

"You know who did this?"

"I have an idea. They just hit my hotel too. I was talking to the police when you called."

"Shit, man, you're in over your head."

Trevor agreed on many levels. "I'm headed that way. I should be in there by nine in the morning."

"And I'll bet you need a ride from the airport."

"Yeah. That would be helpful."

"And in your sick mind I assume you think I'll come get your sorry ass like I owe you for something."

"You do."

"What? For all my shit getting wrecked?"

"For the redhead."

"I told you, this freaked her out."

"I'll talk to her while I'm there."

"Sure," Bryce said and Trevor heard the doubt. "Come home. Do the redhead and then dump her on me. That's a pal."

"Trust me, I'm not going to be doing anything to her."

"Damn. You're totally legit with that girl?"

"Totally," he said, silently laughing at his friend's cluelessness to the world beyond their trashed apartment. "How's my mom?"

"Oh, you know her. She's Sherlock Holmes in a skirt. She'll have the case closed before you get here."

He laughed again. Yeah, he was probably right. "I'll see you tomorrow."

It had grown late and he'd wanted to wait and call Hope when he arrived in New York the next morning, but his phone was ringing before he cleared the turn for the airport. It was Hope's cell phone.

"Hi, baby," he answered softly, hoping not to cause panic.

"Hey. Is everything okay? Do they know who did this?"

"No. They think it was a housekeeper. But I want you to stay with Carissa."

"Yeah, no problem. That's why I'm calling. Thomas said you should come here too." Her voice was sweet, and he already missed her more than he'd ever missed any other person in his life.

"I can't. I'm on my way to New York."

"Right now?" And there was the sound of panic he was trying to avoid.

"I just got a call from my roommate. It seems my office in the city was also broken into."

"Trevor," she whispered and he heard her move about the room and then the door shut. "What's going on?"

"Listen, it's nothing. But I have to check on the office and my apartment. My roommate is a little freaked out."

"Was he at your office?"

"No," he let out a ragged breath. "They hit the apartment too."

"No!" He heard the tears forming in her voice.

"Hey, Hope. I want you to calm down. Please."

"Someone is after you," she said and in the solitude of his car, he shook his head.

No, honey. Someone is after you.

"I'll be okay. I want you to stay with your sister. I'll be back in just a few days. Everything is going to be okay."

"Trevor, when you get back, you stay with me."

"Hope, this isn't the time to go into that."

"Then don't. Know that you're moving in with me. Until everything is settled at least. Then if you think you want a place away from me that's fine. But I'm being firm on this."

He smiled. God, he loved her. He was going to have to make a point to tell her that an awful lot when this mess with Donald Buchanan was over.

"Okay."

"Be careful."

"I promise." He took the exit to the airport. "I have to turn in the car now. I'll call you from New York."

It was his mother standing at the baggage claim when he arrived and not Bryce.

Violet Jacobs smiled at her son, her arms open wide to engulf him in a hug. Trevor smiled as she wrapped her arms around him. He could have picked her up and swung her around, he'd missed her that much.

He took a look at her when he backed away. She was dressed in a business suit and heels. A string of pearls adorned her neck and her perfectly coiffed hair swung just past her jaw. In true fashion of his mother, she interlaced her perfectly French-manicured fingers and raised her eyebrows to him. She didn't say a word, but was asking what's going on?

"I think it's the wife," he said as he hoisted his suitcase from the baggage carousel and walked beside his mother toward the elevator.

"Buchanan's?"

"Yeah." They stepped into the elevator. "He seems to have disappeared."

"He had a heart attack Sunday night. He's still in ICU."

"Bryce figured you'd have this all solved." The elevator opened and they exited to the parking garage.

"Did he?" she asked, her voice playful and knowing.

"So fill me in. What did I get myself into?"

Violet said nothing but simply smiled as they walked toward her BMW parked near the elevator. She hit the key fob and opened the trunk. Trevor lifted his case into the trunk and then walked toward the driver's door and opened it for his mother. She passed by him, patted his cheek, and slid into the car.

Trevor shut the door and took a moment to walk around the car. He let out a breath and then climbed into the passenger seat.

Violet handed him a manila envelope as she drove out of the garage. He opened it and dumped the contents into his lap, then gave a low whistle.

"You work fast."

"Thank you."

"So this is Delores Buchanan?" He examined the photograph, his brows knit.

"That's her."

"In my head this is exactly what I envisioned. Scary."

Violet snickered behind her large dark sunglasses. She paid the parking fee and pulled into traffic.

"So you think I'm right? You think she's the one behind all of this?

"She's looking for that girl you're smitten with."

"Head over heels in love, Mom."

Violet nodded. "You never were one to wait on things when you wanted them. Does she feel the same way?"

"I think she does, but the family is leery of me."

"Who wouldn't open their arms for my son? He's such a good boy," she said in a patronizing tone.

"The family who watches out too closely for her." He lifted his head and turned toward his mother. "They all know she asked me to help find out about her birth parents. Hardest part is keeping my confidentiality for Buchanan. And up until now he's asked me to get to know her, paid me up front, in cash, but doesn't want his wife to know. So here I am playing secretive boyfriend and the sister knows I know too much."

"Oh, you are in so deep." She was laughing, which meant she wasn't worried. He hoped that Hope and Carissa would laugh too when the truth came out.

"Anyway, why is Mrs. Scary Buchanan looking for my Hope?"

"I think she's the reason your Hope lives with her biological sister and her father."

"Run that by me again."

She smiled her in-fact-I-do-have-it-all-figured-out smile. "From what I can pull together, your client had an affair with a woman twenty-four years ago."

"Not news," he said with a rise of his brows.

"Smart-ass, do you want help?" He nodded. She continued, "Somewhere in all this sneaking around the wife got involved, found out about the mistress, confronted the mistress and not the husband. So whatever went down between Scary Buchanan and your girlfriend's biological mother landed Hope in the hands of the family she grew up with."

"You think she threatened Mandy?"

"Yes, that's what I think."

"And why is it that you sell auto, home, and life?" he joked as he fingered his way through the papers on his lap.

His office was trashed too. Every file had been dumped, every drawer emptied, and the water cooler smashed against the wall. Whoever had come looking hadn't found what he was looking for.

"I told you it was a mess," Bryce complained. "How the hell are we going to pay for this?"

"I know for a fact you have a good insurance agent," Trevor joked as he walked through the mess toward his desk.

His letter opener had been stabbed into the wood as though the culprit had taken his revenge on the desk. He shook his head as he tugged the letter opener free.

"Scary Buchanan didn't do this on her own. She has people working for her." He looked around. "I need to find out why."

"Why? She's an overprotective bitch! Her husband fucked around on her, and obviously it's the fault of the floozy."

"Nice thinking, huh?"

Bryce shrugged. "That's how some people think."

"So why has she been quiet for twenty-three years?"

"There wasn't a threat until you came along."

"I didn't just come along." Trevor looked up at Bryce. "He came to me."

"Then there's a reason. If his wife made the mistress disappear, then something got his attention to tell him there was a child."

Bryce was a moron most days, but he was a brilliant puzzle solver.

"So what I need to find out is who contacted him."

"Duh!"

Trevor laughed, picked up his chair from the floor, and sat down at his disheveled desk. "So Buchanan can't keep secrets very well. Wife found out about the mistress, and nearly a quarter of a century later she finds out he hired me to find the child he didn't know about."

Bryce nodded. "Yep."

"And he's not going to be much help since he's in the hospital."

"She try to kill him?"

"I don't know. Mom said he had a heart attack and is in ICU."

"And you're thinking that if he's in ICU his wife is dutifully sitting by his side and you can go ask her yourself."

"You are one amazing son of a bitch." Trevor grinned. "Let's go."

Bryce had a way with people—or a keen skill in lying. The cute young nurse at the station was baffled by the bull he'd produced that he and Trevor were sons of a previous marriage and wanted to see their father. By the end of the conversation, Bryce had touched her hand, complimented her on her hair, had her phone number, and Trevor was walking through the curtain to see Donald Buchanan.

Buchanan lay unconscious. His ICU bay was empty of visitors.

The nurse, hot on Bryce's trail, followed them into the bay. "He had bypass surgery yesterday, so he's still out. But his vitals are good," she said as she checked the monitors by his side. "I can't let you stay long, but…"

"Where's his wife?" Trevor asked.

The nurse shrugged. "She left after the surgery and said she'd be out of town for a few days."

That caught Trevor in the gut. Where would she have to go while her beloved was dying? "Did she say where she was going?"

The young nurse shook her head. "She only left a number in case we needed to get in touch with her."

Trevor looked at Bryce. How to get the number? The nurse would be suspicious of two guys who claimed not to know the cell number of their stepmother. "See, I told you we should have told her we were coming."

Bryce shrugged his shoulders. "Sorry, bro. My mistake."

Ah, he was good, Trevor thought. But that still didn't get them the number. Unless... "The phone number she gave you, is it her new cell phone number?"

"Oh, I don't know if it's a new number."

"Probably is. She lost her old phone and had to get a new one. Didn't even think to keep the old number. You know how stepmothers are. They only think of themselves."

The nurse nodded. "I can get it for you."

"Would you?" Bryce smiled with a wink and one more touch on the arm of the baffled nurse. "We'd really appreciate that. You might be able to tell, she doesn't accept us much."

"I understand." The nurse shook her head. "My stepmother is the same way. I'm not her child, but she seems to forget I'm the child of her husband."

"Exactly," Trevor added. "We'll leave him rest if you can get us that number."

"Oh, sure." She smiled and walked out of the room.

Bryce and Trevor exchanged glances before the nurse returned with the number.

"Thanks." Bryce smiled as he put the number in his shirt pocket. "I really appreciate it. I'll give you a call, okay?"

"Great. Bye." She gave him a flirty wave and Trevor shook his head.

"Let's get out of here," he whispered as they hurried out of the hospital.

Hope blew out a ragged breath as Thomas made his third walk through the store in as many hours.

"You're going to start scaring away my guests." She huffed.

"Customers. And I'm just looking out for you. This has me freaked out and it should have you freaked out too."

"This has nothing to do with me, Thomas."

"He has something to do with you." His eyebrows were raised in warning.

"You sound like my sister."

"For good reason." He moved in and hugged her, placing a kiss on the top of her head. "I like Trevor. Don't get me wrong. But if he's into something where someone is hitting him from the front, back, and side…I don't want you involved."

Hoped tapped her foot and frowned. "Thomas, I am involved." She grabbed the lapel of his sports coat and gave it a tug. "I love him," she whispered.

"I know you do, and that's why I want to keep you safe." He gave her hand a pat as the door opened to the store. "I'll be back in an hour."

She shook her head with a laugh. "Okay." She watched as he walked out the door and then she turned to the woman who had walked in. "Hi."

"Hello," she said back in a cool and precise tone.

"Can I help you find anything specific?" Hope asked as she moved behind the counter.

"Oh, I'm just in town visiting an old friend and I saw your store. I just thought I'd poke my head in." The woman took a sweeping look of the walls. "Are you the artist who does all the painting?"

"Yes. It's my passion."

"My late husband was an artist. He worked with all mediums."

"I prefer oils, but I do have a lot of fun with watercolors and charcoals as you can see." Hope smiled, pleased with her own talents.

"Is your father or mother an artist?"

"No. My father is a retired airline pilot and my mother teaches cello. But she used to tour with Pablo DiAngelo before I was born."

The woman nodded, and Hope felt a pang of disappointment. Usually the mere mention that her mother toured with the vocal legend had people smiling and commenting on how they loved his voice and his music. But this woman wasn't impressed.

"Can I offer you something to drink?" Hope asked, finally remembering her policy of guest versus customers.

"Oh, no thank you. I must be going. Will you be open tomorrow?" The woman pushed her black purse into the crook of her arm and raised her brows as she waited for Hope to answer.

"Yes. I open at ten."

"Wonderful. I think I'll stop by then and look around again."

The woman walked toward the door, her black high heels tapping out an uncomfortable beat against the tile floor.

When the door closed, Hope let out a breath. Customers who walked in off the street didn't make Hope uncomfortable, but that woman had. She wouldn't at all be disappointed if the woman didn't return.

Trevor pulled into traffic and headed into town. "We have to find her."

"Already on it. Head south. Their house is only eight miles away," Bryce said, never looking up from his iPhone.

"What are you doing?"

"Cross referencing the phone number, you ass. How do you do your job?" He peeked at him from over his sunglasses.

"I guess I rely on you and my mother to do it for me."

"Duh! Again, I say, duh!"

That made Trevor laugh. He was going to miss Bryce when he moved to Kansas City to be with Hope. The very thought made him smile. And then panic filled his body. He wanted to get this solved and get back to her. He didn't want anything happening to her while he was gone. But just to make sure, and not alarm her, he called Thomas.

"Things are normal." Thomas sounded tense. "She's pissed at me because I've been over there every hour since she opened and I made her drive with me to work today."

"Thanks for taking care of her. I really don't think there's anything for her to worry about…"

"But you want to make sure."

"Yes." He was grateful that Thomas understood. "Don't tell her I called. She'll get mad if I check in on her too."

"She's as stubborn as her sister, and that, my friend, doesn't get shared either."

"Lips are sealed."

"Good. Be careful, Trevor."

"Thanks. Bye."

He pulled in front of the brownstone that matched the address Bryce had found.

"I was expecting something bigger." Bryce removed his glasses.

"It's what's inside." Trevor pulled the keys from the ignition and they both headed up the steps.

Trevor rang the doorbell, but there was no answer. There was no movement. Cupping his hand around his eyes, Trevor tried to peer into the windows, but the drapes were drawn.

"Yep, she's outta town," Bryce said with a cluck of his tongue. "Maybe she's already out spending her husband's money."

"Husband's money," Trevor said as he headed back to the car.

"Oh, you have a light bulb over your head." Bryce pulled open his door and slid into the car. "What's up?"

Trevor started the car. "He paid me six thousand dollars to get to know his daughter."

"And she just found out it was missing?"

"And sent to my hotel."

"Damn, look at you with all the women chasing you." Bryce put his sunglasses back on. "Now where are we going?"

"While we're in the city we're going to make one more stop and talk to one more woman."

"Yeah, you're going to talk to the redhead, whose name is Patricia, by the way."

"Okay, so I have two stops." Trevor grunted as he headed toward Ruth Marlow's house.

One of the things Trevor had learned about Mandy Marlow was that she never got far from home, no matter where she called home at the time.

Ruth Marlow's modest home was a mere twenty minutes from the home of Donald Buchanan's.

Trevor stood at the door. His mouth had gone dry. He'd spoken to Ruth Marlow before, and Carissa had warned him that she was a nasty woman. So he knew he was taking his life into his own hands by showing up on her doorstep.

The moment she opened the door he knew he had the right house. As eerie as it was, Hope's eyes stared back at him from behind lids that were aged by years and smoking.

Hope also carried her biological grandmother's stature. Short and curvy.

"Yes?" Her voice was softer than he'd remembered it to be when he'd spoken to her and he was very afraid to tell her who he was.

"Ruth Marlow?"

"Who's asking?" Her eyes narrowed and suddenly she didn't look like Hope at all.

"We spoke on the phone a month or so ago. My name is Trevor Jacobs."

Her eyes flew open with the mention of his name and her lips pursed. "Mr. Jacobs, I told you last month that I had nothing more to tell you."

"Yes," he said quickly. "And I know you don't want to talk about your daughter, but I have a feeling that she is in danger and I need some more information."

She didn't talk right away. "This long and she's still causing problems for her children she gave up?"

"Mrs. Marlow," he said softly, knowing he had only one piece of evidence that perhaps Ruth didn't know about since she carried such disdain for her own daughter. "Are you aware that Mandy died some twenty-three years ago?"

She held the door open and backed into the house offering him a silent invitation. He glanced back at the car to Bryce to give him a solemn nod.

Ruth walked toward the back of the house to the small kitchen and she sat down at the table by the window. Her eyes had grown distant and her shoulders hunched.

"Are you all right?" Trevor asked as he pulled out the chair across from her and took a seat. She nodded. "Did you know she died?"

Ruth looked up at him, her eyes moist with tears that refused to fall. "I heard, but I don't think I believed it."

"Why would you not believe news like that?"

She shrugged. "You didn't know Mandy."

Trevor nodded and eased back into his chair, waiting for her to speak.

"I told you the last time I'd seen her she came here with a baby. She was eighteen years old and she was looking for money." She pulled a napkin from the holder on the table and dabbed at her eyes. "When I received the letter that said she'd died, I assumed she was trying to scam more money."

"Someone sent you a letter about her death?"

"Yes. A woman. Let's see…" She shook her head and frowned. "K. Birdman, Burkman…"

"Burkhalter?" Trevor asked, his heart racing in his chest.

"Burkhalter." She smiled. "Yes, that was it. K. Burkhalter."

"Just K? No name?"

"No. But the writing was distinctively female and, from what I could tell, I would venture to guess old."

Trevor could hardly breathe. Hope's own grandmother had contacted Mandy's mother.

"May I ask you what the letter said exactly?"

"Well it said something about her having another baby. And that the baby would be safe and living with her sister. Mandy's other baby, I assumed. Though they would have been many, many years apart. I figured it was vague enough that she'd put someone up to it to get money. I didn't realize this person was telling the truth."

"Had she ever contacted you after she came looking for money?"

"Mandy? No. But that girl she had did once. Maybe twenty-five years ago. I told her to go away and never call me again. Mandy was using her to get to me."

"She said that?" He lifted his brows. The conversation he'd had with Carissa was quite different.

"Well… No. I guess she didn't really say that. She said she was Mandy's daughter and she wanted to meet me."

"Mrs. Marlow, I didn't come to tell you your daughter died. I'm very sorry that this is how you had to find out the truth."

"Why are you here, then, if she's not after money?"

He blew out a ragged breath. "She did have another daughter, twenty-three years ago. She had an affair with a married man and the baby was a product of that. Does the name Donald Buchanan ring a bell to you?"

Ruth's head lifted and her eyes widened. "Donald Buchanan?" Trevor nodded. "Well yes, I know who he is. He was my husband's business partner forty years ago."

Trevor's head began to spin. The world was becoming a much smaller place, and all of his answers seemed to lie with Ruth Marlow.

"So you are familiar with Delores Buchanan?"

"Nasty bitch," she said with a shake of her head. "I never did like her."

"When was the last time you saw her?"

"Not too long ago really, maybe a month ago. She ran into me at the antique store my niece runs. My niece had gone to lunch and I was covering for her. She came in as if she owned the place with her little black purse and red nail polish. She asked me about my husband and I told her he died some years back, but now that I think about it, Donald was at the funeral. She would have known that." She lifted her head.

He could feel his tongue swell. Things were falling quickly into place. "How long ago, exactly did your husband die?"

"Twenty-four years ago," she said as her voice drifted off. "Oh dear, God. Mandy must have known that and been there, though I didn't see her."

Trevor shrugged. "Was Delores there?"

"No. She didn't get along with my husband or me for that matter. But Donald was there. Do you think Mandy was trying to get money from the company after my husband died? She had to have known Donald would assume the other half of the company. I never had an interest in the company."

"I don't have those answers, Mrs. Marlow. All I know is that Donald Buchanan is in the hospital recovering from bypass surgery and his wife has left town. I also know that about a month ago he came to my office to ask me to find Mandy."

"He didn't know she had died either?"

Trevor shook his head. "Somehow he'd come into the knowledge that there might have been a child born from their affair."

Ruth nodded. "I am so sorry that my daughter could stir up so much trouble."

"With all due respect, I don't think she's stirred up any problems. I think either Donald or Delores Buchanan have something to hide, and I have to figure out what it is before they get to Hope."

"Hope?" she asked, and Trevor realized he'd been thinking aloud.

"I'm sorry. I didn't mean to mention…"

"Is that the daughter of Mandy and Donald?" she asked, and Trevor nodded. Brightness came into her eyes and her lips softened into a thin smile. "What is her sister's name?"

"Carissa."

Ruth nodded. "She called me once."

"So you said."

"I wasn't very nice to her. Maybe I should have been."

"You had your reasons. If it's any consolation to you, they were raised by a fine man."

"Do I know him?"

He gave some thought to telling her his name, but he couldn't help but like the woman who had once made him fear the very thought of doing his job. "David Kendal."

Her eyes opened wide again. "David Kendal is Carissa's father?"

"You know him?"

"He flew for the charter company my husband and Donald used all the time. My husband was very fond of him. That would have been where Mandy met him. We'd often meet him when his plane would come in. David Kendal was one of my husband's favorite pilots."

"You were unaware that he was the father of your daughter's first child?"

"We were very upset. I don't suppose it would have mattered much then," she said as she looked out the window next to her. "You know Mandy's daughters?"

"Yes, ma'am."

"And they are good people?"

"I don't think you'd find better."

She kept her stare out the window. He watched her as she chewed on her lip. "She was an artist, my Mandy. Did you know that?" Trevor shook his head. "So was Donald if I remember correctly," she added. "When she was twelve she won a district art competition." The tears were back, but the look was different. There was joy in her face. She'd remembered something good about the daughter she'd all but forgotten about.

"Mrs. Marlow." He cleared his throat. "Would you be interested in meeting the girls?"

"Oh, no," she answered quickly. "No. They don't need me in their lives. I've always blamed myself for the way

Mandy turned out. I couldn't suddenly show up and say 'Hi, I'm your grandmother.' I'm sure they had a wonderful grandmother."

K. Burkhalter, Trevor thought. From what he'd heard, she was a wonderful grandmother.

"If you change your mind, or if you think of any other reason Donald or Delores Buchanan might have gone looking for Mandy, would you call me?" He took his business card from his pocket and handed it to her.

"I will."

"Thank you." Trevor stood and Ruth followed.

"Mr. Jacobs, I'd like to give you something. Would you mind waiting a moment?"

"I can wait." Trevor watched her slowly walk down the hallway to what he assumed was a bedroom.

Ruth wasn't gone long and when she returned she carried with her a box. It wasn't a large box, but the way she carried it he knew it was full.

"This is all I have left of the Mandy I knew before she dropped out of school and became the woman I've tried so hard to forget," she said, guilt plaguing the very sound of her voice.

She set the box down on a table in the entryway and opened it. "I would like you to take this to her daughters if you don't mind."

"May I?" Trevor asked nodding toward the box for approval to search through it.

"Of course."

Inside the box were pictures of a little girl looking up at him who remarkably looked like one of Carissa's daughters. He couldn't remember which one, but the face was the same. She was swimming, holding a sparkler on the Fourth of July, and sitting on her father's knee in the pictures. The ribbon from the art show her mother had told him about was in the box along with small trinkets and memorabilia from Mandy's youth.

"Are you sure you want to part with these?"

"Yes. I'm sure whatever those girls know about Mandy isn't good. Maybe this will shed some light on who she started out as."

And that, he thought as he assured her they would appreciate it, was what Hope had been looking for.

Chapter Eight

Hope turned off the lights in the store as Thomas and Carissa walked through the door.

"Ready to go?" Carissa stepped inside.

"Yes. Will you at least let me go by my place and get a few things?" Hope pleaded.

"Of course. But I'm going in with you," Carissa demanded.

"I wouldn't have expected anything else." She followed Thomas and her sister out and locked the door behind them.

"Does this look familiar?" Thomas stood at the curb by the car, holding a wrinkled piece of paper that had a tire track on it. He handed it to Hope.

She studied it and felt the pang of guilt pierce her chest when she realized it was one of Trevor's lists. Unwilling to share any more information, Hope folded it and tucked it into her purse and hoped there would be no more questions about it. "It must be something Trevor dropped when he left yesterday. I'll talk to him about it when he gets home." She opened the door to the car and climbed in back.

She hated keeping secrets from her sister. And how careless of Trevor to drop such an important piece of information. She'd give him some credit; he was rushing out when he'd left.

Thomas pulled to the curb in front of Hope's apartment and parked the car.

"Why don't you wait for us? We'll be right out." Carissa gave her husband a quick kiss along with the instruction before she climbed from the car. Hope followed her toward the apartment and let them in.

As soon as Hope turned on the light Carissa put her hand out. "Let me see it."

"See what?"

"The paper Thomas found. What are you two up to?"

Hope huffed out a breath and shook her head. She reached into her purse and pulled out the paper.

"These are phone numbers and addresses of banks." Carissa glanced at her.

"In the things that I have that were Mandy's, we found a key to a safe-deposit box."

"A safe-deposit box? Why would someone like her have one of those?"

Hope shrugged. "That's what we're trying to find out. Just a little piece to our puzzle."

"Where's the key?"

Hope hesitated. "In the box on the table."

She led Carissa to the table, where the box she and Trevor had gone through still sat. She pulled out the key and the piece of paper from the wallet and handed them to Carissa. Her sister was frowning at the paper. "Is this an account number?"

"I don't know. That was what Trevor was trying to find out when he left."

"Hope." She looked up. "Do you think this is why Trevor's room was broken into?"

"What could be so important that they would break into houses and hotel rooms? She didn't have anything."

Carissa tapped her foot and bit at her lip. "Listen. I talked to Trevor about Mandy's mother. If he's looking into some of those leads, maybe someone realized he knew something about Mandy. Maybe Mandy had something."

Hope's eyes flew open wide. "You're talking to Trevor about Mandy? I thought you didn't want me to do this." Anger shook in her voice with the betrayal of her sister's confession.

"I just wanted him to be careful about who he sought out."

"Wait." Hope held her hand up to her sister. "You knew who Mandy's mother was?"

Carissa cringed. "Hope, this isn't important."

"Like hell it isn't." She took the key from her sister and the piece of paper that Trevor had written on. "You can't tell me not to find these people when you already know about them. That's not fair."

"Hope, let it go."

"No! How do you know Mandy's mother? I thought you didn't know anyone but Mandy."

"I didn't. I mean I don't." She blew out a ragged breath. "Listen, when I was fifteen I looked up her mother. Yes, I wanted to know there was more to her than the coke addict who ditched me." A crease formed in her forehead as her brows drew together. "Anyway, I called Mandy's mother. She was mean and rude. She told me to never contact her again and then she hung up on me."

"That's it?"

"That's it." Carissa took a step closer to her. "Listen, if Trevor contacted her, then maybe she came after him."

"Some seventy-year-old lady is going to go about destroying his home and office?"

"Maybe not personally."

Hope nodded. "We need to find that safe-deposit box."

"What about Trevor?"

"He won't be back until Saturday morning. We have one day to do this."

Carissa pressed the palm of her hand to her forehead and rubbed. "Okay. But we don't tell Thomas. He'll freak out if he knows I decided to help you."

Hope's smiled, grateful to have Carissa's help. "You never have let me down."

"I don't plan to start either, no matter how I feel about doing this. C'mon. Get your stuff and get what you need of Mandy's, and let's go."

Trevor sat at the kitchen table with his father and Bryce. They each took pulls from their beers as they studied the cards in their hands.

"Who dealt this?" Brandon Jacobs shook his head.

"That would be you, old man."

"Watch it, Bryce, or you'll wake up naked in the ditch with no sign of your money."

"There is already no sign of my money," he whined, and Brandon laughed. "Okay, slacker." He nodded toward Trevor. "You in or out?"

"Out." He threw his cards on the table, picked up his beer, and paced the kitchen.

"This is no fun if you're not in with us." Brandon set down his cards. "What's wrong, son?"

"Nothing."

"He misses his girlfriend." Bryce threw down his cards and swigged his beer. "I think we need to take him out back and beat him, just for the sport."

Brandon raised his brows in consideration.

"You'll do no such thing." Violet walked through the kitchen, slapping Bryce on the back of the head. "He's allowed to miss her."

"Thanks, Mom."

Violet smiled and patted his cheek. "So is that what's wrong? You miss your girlfriend?" she asked in the same patronizing tone Bryce had used, and they laughed at Trevor's expense.

He shook his head and finished his beer. Then he said quietly, "Yeah. I really do."

"Well, you patched things up with the redhead. I guess you can go back." Bryce rolled his eyes at him.

"Thanks," he said with a nod in Bryce's direction. "But I'm staying there."

"Shit. I thought you'd changed your mind."

"You're moving to Kansas City?" Violet opened the refrigerator and took out a beer. She handed it to Trevor, who opened it for her and passed it back. She took a sip, her eyes still steady on his.

"I am. It's where I want to be. I want to be with her, Mom."

She nodded and then a smile slid across her lips. "For some reason when you took this case I knew you were never coming back. Fate is a strong thing."

"I know."

"As long as you're happy."

"I am."

"Great." Bryce lifted his beer. "Your dad has all my money. Your girl gets you for a roommate, and what do I have?"

"A new lead on a hit and run?" Violet interjected.

"You have a job for me?" When she nodded, he jerked his thumb over his shoulder and grinned at Trevor. "Go, asshole. Mom will take care of me now. She always did love me more." Bryce winked at Violet.

Brandon slapped him on the back of the head just as Violet had done earlier. "Better deal another hand of cards so I can take more of your money, and then you can think about winking at my wife again."

Hope watched her sister take command of the morning ritual at their home from her place at the kitchen table. Thomas hadn't questioned Carissa when she'd instructed him to take the kids to school, the little ones to her mother's, and get to work early. As soon as he left, Carissa dropped a box on the kitchen table. Hope watched silently as her sister filled a cup of coffee then piled her hair atop her head and secured it with band before sitting down at the table.

Hope gave a nod to the box. "What is this?"

"It's what I have."

Carissa took the lid off the box, and Hope leaned forward to look inside. There were a handful of photographs of Carissa as a little girl. A few scribbled drawings she'd made with crayons.

Carissa pulled out a large envelope, which was tucked inside. She handed it to Hope.

"Dad gave this to me when I was eighteen. It's between you and me now. I don't think he ever even told Mom about it."

Hope opened the envelope with shaky fingers and let the contents slide onto the table. She let out a sigh. It was another secret between her family.

There was the original copy of Mandy's death certificate, copies of the newspaper clippings from her death notices, and two envelopes with Carissa's name on them.

"What are these?" Hope held up the envelopes.

"This one is a letter from Katie," she said as she took the envelope with their grandmother's handwriting on it. "She wrote it about the time you were born, but I didn't get it until she died. Mom found it in her things."

Carissa opened the letter and scanned her eyes over it before handing it to Hope.

My Dearest Carissa,

Today you became my legal great-granddaughter. I am so pleased to call you that, though I have felt that you held that place in my heart since you arrived when you were seven years old. Now we have your sister too, and I consider myself doubly blessed. I want you to know how much I love you and I want you to make sure your sister knows how much I love her too. I may not be around long enough to let her know myself.

Hope wiped at the tears that had run down her face, and looked up to see Carissa wiping her eyes too.

"Yes, I'm crying. I know what the damn thing says," she said with a smile. Carissa nodded to the letter. "Keep going."

I wanted to tell you that I've done something, and perhaps it was a mistake, but I thought you should know. After Hope's birth and your mother's death, I wrote to Mandy's mother and told her that Mandy had died. I thought she might have liked to know. I told her that she'd had another baby too.

As of yet I haven't heard from her.

The reason I'm telling you this is in case my fate to join my Charlie and my dearest friend Millie is soon, I wanted you to know what I'd done. If Mrs. Marlow comes looking for you, you'll know how she found you.

I don't know how anyone could know they have granddaughters as wonderful as you and your sister and not want to meet you. I suppose that is her loss and my gain.

I love you and your sister very much. I want only the best for you both.

Love,
Grandma Katie

Hope put the letter down in front of her and ran her fingers over it. She swallowed the last of her tears, missing her great-grandmother.

"So Mandy's mother knows about us?"

Carissa nodded. "Feeling a little let down?"

Hope shrugged. She wasn't sure what to feel.

"Here," Carissa said, handing her the other envelope. "This one's from Dad."

Hope opened the envelope with their father's handwriting on the front.

Carissa scooted her chair closer to Hope. "Since Mandy died a few months before I turned eighteen, he waited to close out some of her things. He turned power of attorney over to me so I could do it. I think he thought it would help me not be so angry at her. That's the book to her savings account. When I closed it out there was enough money for me to go to college on."

Hope remained silent and again her hands began to shake.

Carissa let out a breath. "I took the money. I was mad. That's how I paid for college because I felt she owed it to me. She'd pawned me off from the moment I was born until I found Dad, and then she vanished a few years later. I thought I'd take what I could. But Hope, I never thought to find out why she had that much money in her account."

"Do you think this is where the safe-deposit box is?"

"It would be a great place to start looking. And…" She smiled. "The bank isn't in Kansas City, so Trevor might have never found it."

"Where's the bank?"

"Jefferson City."

Hope listened as Carissa made the phone call to the bank where she'd closed out Mandy's accounts almost twenty-three years ago. The man on the phone confirmed the number Carissa had read to him was an account number, but without identification and proof of power of attorney, he wouldn't confirm that the number belonged to Mandy.

Carissa reached for Hope's hand and gave it a squeeze. "We have a two-and-a-half-hour drive ahead of us. We should make it by one o'clock."

Hope nodded. Her mouth had gone dry.

Twenty minutes from Jefferson City, Hope's phone rang. Carissa shook her head before Hope answered the phone. "Don't tell him what we're doing. Not yet."

Hope nodded, then answered. "Hello, handsome."

"I called your shop. Your mom said she was covering for you today. Are you okay?" There was a hint of worry in his voice and she didn't like it.

"I'm fine. Carissa and I are spending the day together. You know, girl stuff."

"Sounds nice. I had some man time myself last night. Cost me fifty bucks. Hurts more when you play cards and lose to your own father."

Hope laughed. She was missing him terribly. "When do you get in tomorrow?"

"Ten. I know you're working so I'll either get a car or a cab."

"Dad said he'd cover for me. I'll be there. I've missed you too much not to be waiting for you."

"I never thought I'd have someone who longed to pick me up from the airport."

"You have me," she said softly then said goodbye as Carissa took the exit from the highway that would lead them toward the bank.

"Keep your eyes peeled," Carissa instructed as she slowly drove down the street in search of the bank. "Some of these buildings weren't here twenty-three years ago."

"So, seriously, there was enough money for you to go through school on?"

"Seriously. There was over a hundred thousand in the account when I closed it. I never told Dad just how much was in there. I put a lot of it away, paid my way through school, and when I was ready to open the school I used the money I had left to put a down payment on the building."

That was a lot of money for a woman who'd lived in a cheap motel.

"There it is," Carissa said as she made the turn into the parking lot.

Hope's heart rate picked up as they neared the bank. "I'm afraid to go in here."

"Why? She can't hurt us know."

Hope nodded and turned to her sister. "What do we do if we find something?"

"Then we deal with it." She covered Hope's hand with hers. "Whatever we find is only material and belongs to someone who didn't care about us. Let's go see what it is."

Hope nodded in agreement and then raised her hand to the charm that hung from her neck. The Saint Nicholas medal had kept her mother, sister, and her safe for years. She gave it a squeeze, hoping it would still work even though she was grown.

Peter Westfall met them in the lobby of the bank and escorted them to his office.

"I have her death certificate as well as the power of attorney papers with me," Carissa said as she laid them on his desk. "She had an account here that I closed, about twenty-three years ago."

"But you didn't close out the safe-deposit box?"

"I didn't know about it until we found the key. I don't even know if it's from this bank. It was just a place to start."

"The number you gave me this morning on the phone did match a box we have here. Do you have the key with you?"

Hope reached into her purse and pulled it out. She set it on the desk and Peter Westfall nodded.

"Wonderful. Well, let me get the other key and we'll go into the vault and get your box."

He left them in the office while he went for the other key. Hope grabbed for Carissa's hand. "Why am I so scared?"

"It's okay. Maybe the box is empty," Carissa offered as Peter returned to the office and they followed him out.

They followed the man into the vault, passing a security guard at the door. Peter put in the key from the bank, and Carissa, with shaky hands, inserted the other key into the box. Each of them turned their keys and the box slid into Peter's hands. He handed the box to Carissa.

Carissa shot Hope a glance and she knew it wasn't empty.

Peter showed them to an adjacent room where they could open the box and go through it in private. He left them to the contents, shutting the door behind him.

Both women stood and looked down and the closed box. Hope didn't want to be the first to see what their birth mother was hiding.

"Okay." Carissa blew out a breath. "Here we go."

She slowly slid the lid from the box and Hope held her breath. Inside the safe-deposit box were stock certificates. Carissa pulled them out and laid them to the side. There was another bundle of money and a letter addressed to "My Daughters."

Carissa lifted the letter out of the box and her hands, unsteady and shaking, rattled the envelope.

They exchanged glances again.

"Open it. Fast," Hope said, her own lip quivering.

Carissa started to run her finger through the envelope that bared the name of the bank. She pulled the letter from the envelope and the letterhead had the name of the bank as well.

She cleared her throat and began.

To My Beautiful Daughters,

As I write this, I am sitting in a little room at the bank filling this safe-deposit box that I hope someday you will find. I know that I will never return here.

I am seven months pregnant with a baby that I know will be a girl. I am headed to Kansas City to give birth to her and convince a wonderful man to raise her. I have done all I can to ensure that he will be able to take her without problems. I have changed my name to match his, and if I can convince him to be her father, he will only have to carry her out of the hospital and give her a wonderful life.

I was told that if I carried the baby to term I would die. I feel weak and I'm sure this to be very true. I have stopped taking my medications because after she is born, I do not want to live.

I have chosen a path for my life that has left me unhappy. I have disgraced my family and have lost all connection to them.

Carissa, if you are reading this, please know that I did love you. You were an amazing gift to me that I didn't respect.

She stopped reading, took a breath, and wiped her eyes. Hope gave her a nod and urged her to continue.

I know since I walked away from you, leaving you with your father, you've blossomed into a beautiful woman. I've heard you play your cello and I've seen you turn into a beautiful woman. I've never been too far away.

"Oh, God!" Carissa handed the letter to Hope. "Finish this," she said.

Hope nodded and took the letter.

The baby I am carrying is your sister. And I hope that you and your father will consider raising her so that you will be together. This baby will need her family. I will be gone, and her father does not know about her.

I've done something I'm not proud of. I had an affair with a married man. He's someone I've known my whole life. He was my father's business partner.

Hope looked up from the letter, realizing Mandy had told them who her birth father was. Even without a name they had somewhere to start looking.

He gave me the stocks for the company because he felt I was owed them after my father died. I hope they will be worth something to you someday. The other money that I have put into an account, and what I have stored here, was given to me by his wife to stay away from him and never mention the baby. I have sunk low enough to have accepted her bribe and to have run away. I was afraid that if I didn't disappear, she would have had me killed and that would have killed my baby too.

I know I will die, but I want my baby to live.

Hope stopped and put her hand to her chest. "She was protecting me."

Carissa nodded. "She'd cleaned up. I know her conscience played a big role in her giving you to us, but I didn't know someone had paid her off to do it."

"I'm glad they did," Hope said, covering her sister's hand with her own. She took a deep breath and continued to read the letter.

Carissa, I'm sorry for everything I have ever done. To have been fair to you I should have told David about you from the start and let him have you. He wanted to keep you and I lied to him. I hurt you and I'm so very sorry. I hope you can accept my apology.

Please take care of my baby and love her. She is your sister and I know that will mean something to you.

I love you both. I'm sorry I will never get to know the baby that grows inside of me. I'm sure if all goes well and she is raised a Kendal she will be perfect too.

Love, Mandy

They both sat silently. Hope tried to hold back the wall of tears, and watched as her sister did the same, but eventually they broke through.

Carissa blew out a ragged breath. "She didn't even sign the letter, Mom," she said with a shake of her head. "Let's get out of here." She took the stocks and cash and slid them into her purse.

Hope took the letter, put it into the envelope, and carried them out with her. It was the first time in her life she felt a connection to Mandy Marlow, and she wasn't sure what to do with the feeling.

They drove home in silence. Hope tried to make sense of the words of a woman who had been dead for twenty-three years. And from Carissa's tapping of her fingers on the steering wheel she assumed she was doing the same.

Hope had counted the cash that Mandy had left in the box. There was ten thousand dollars. Neither of them had staked claim to the money or the stocks. Hope was sure she didn't want the responsibility of Mandy's last gift.

Trevor put his suitcase into his mother's car and stood at the curb waiting for her. In a few hours he'd be in the arms of the woman he loved. He'd never have thought he could miss a woman so much, but he missed Hope completely.

"Do you have everything?" Violet asked as she locked the front door.

"Yeah."

"Is she picking you up when you get there?"

He smiled. "Yes. Her father is watching the store so she can be at the airport." He walked to the driver's side of the car and opened the door for his mother.

"You are bringing her here to meet me, right?"

"Of course. For your birthday."

With a rise of her brows she looked at him over her sunglasses. "That's only a few weeks away. You'll be flying in then too?"

"Is there a problem?"

"Not at all," she said, patting his cheek with her hand as she slid into the seat, and Trevor shut the door.

At the airport, Violet pulled to the curb and met Trevor at the back of the car.

"I feel like this goodbye is so permanent." Her voice cracked, and it gave a tug at Trevor's chest.

"I'm sorry, Mom."

Violet slapped him on the shoulder and took off her sunglasses. "I'm your mother. I'm allowed to feel the disappointment of losing my only son." She took a deep breath, lifting her shoulders and dropping them again. "But my baby is in love." She clasped her hands to her chest. "He's in love." This time a smile brightened her face.

"I am." His grin was so huge it hurt. "She'll love you too."

"Of course she will." Violet kissed her son on the cheek. "Be happy."

"I will."

"Be careful."

On a sigh he said, "I will."

Trevor picked up his suitcase and the box that Ruth Marlow had given him. He kissed his mother once more and disappeared into the airport to make his journey back to Hope.

Just as he passed through security and found his gate he opened his phone to call Hope, but it rang in his hands.

"Jacobs," he answered as he set the box down on the seat next to him.

"Mr. Jacobs, it's Ruth Marlow."

"Mrs. Marlow, I didn't expect to hear from you." He sat up in the seat. "How can I help you?"

"Well, after you were here I did some looking around. I got to thinking about Delores Buchanan."

"And you remembered something?"

"Yes." He heard her take a deep breath. "When my husband died, Donald Buchanan bought back my husband's shares of the company from me. I had no use for them. My husband had set us up to live nicely through retirement. So I sold them to him. But when Delores cornered me in the antique store last month, she asked me about my stocks for the company."

Trevor's heart began to race. "She didn't know her husband bought them back from you?"

"That's how it sounded. But that was a very long time ago. Maybe she forgot. Anyway, I just thought I'd let you know I remembered that part of the conversation."

"I appreciate it very much. Again, if you think of anything…"

"I'll be sure to let you know." She didn't say goodbye right away, and just as Trevor took a breath to speak Ruth asked, "Are you on your way back to her?"

"Yes. She'll be picking me up at the airport."

"I assume she and her sister are beautiful. My Mandy was beautiful once. Drugs and alcohol changed how she looked, but once she was very pretty."

"Both of her girls are beautiful, Mrs. Marlow. In fact, if you don't mind my saying, when I saw you I could see a lot of Hope in you."

"Really?" Her voice lifted.

"Yes."

"Well, I'm glad they had a nice life."

"Mrs. Marlow, are you sure you don't want to meet them?"

There was a pause and Trevor thought perhaps she'd changed her mind. "No. Take care of them, Mr. Jacobs. I know you love her very much, and that will be nice to know. Goodbye."

"Goodbye, Mrs. Marlow." He closed his phone just as they called for his flight.

Quickly he dialed Hope's phone, but it went straight to voice mail. He closed it again and boarded the plane. In only a few hours, he'd be in her arms.

Twenty minutes until closing, the door to Hope's store opened and the bell rang. David looked up from his crossword puzzle and smiled at the woman who sauntered in. He'd hoped to get away with helping Hope out and not having to have talked to any customers, but it didn't look like that was going to happen.

"Good afternoon. Nice day, isn't it?" he asked with a smile, but the woman coolly looked him over.

"Where is the woman who owns the store?" Her red-painted lips were pursed.

"She had an errand to run. I'm her father. Can I help you with something?"

The woman snorted a laughed and jaunted out her chin. "You are her father?"

"Yes."

He watched as she ran her tongue over her teeth and considered him.

"So you were the first one Mandy Marlow sank her claws into." She clutched the shiny black purse that hung from the crook in her elbow on rhinestone-encrusted straps.

The mere mention of the woman's name had David's skin chill. He stood from his seat to be eye level with the woman who seemed to have secrets hidden behind her dark stare. "Who are you?"

"I am obviously no one. But now that I've seen your face, I remember you."

He studied her, at a disadvantage because he had no idea who she was. "I'm sorry. I don't recall your name," he said, trying to keep his calm.

"You wouldn't. You were too busy knocking up seventeen-year-olds."

Her words stabbed him in the heart. Right where he assumed she was aiming. Whoever the nasty woman was, she was part of his past, but why she was standing in his daughter's store looking for her was beyond him.

"I don't know what you want with my daughter, but I'd appreciate it if you left."

"All I want is what is mine. I'll be back for it." She turned and stalked out the door.

David huffed out a breath and watched as the woman drove away in a taxi that had waited right outside.

Hope was waiting for him at the baggage claim, and the smile on her face told him she missed him as much as he'd missed her.

She ran to him and wrapped her arms around his neck, and the part of him that hadn't felt whole since he'd left her was complete again.

"God, how long were you gone?" She kissed him hard on the mouth and he held her close to him, never wanting to let her go again.

"Too long." He lifted his head back to look at her. "Everything is quiet?"

"Sure." She kissed him again before releasing her grasp on him. "Thomas hasn't let me out of his sight for three days. I've had to go to work with him in the morning, lock up, and go home with him at night. It's like I'm in protective lockdown."

"Well, that's okay." He retrieved his luggage and with his arm wrapped around Hope's waist, they started toward the parking garage. "Where is your sister today?"

"Teaching, why?"

"I have something for both of you. But I want you together when I give it to you."

"You brought us a present?"

"You could say that." They reached her car, and Trevor tossed his suitcase into the trunk and gave it a slam. "So does your offer still stand?" he asked as he slid into the car.

"Which one?"

"All of them," he said with a wink and she smiled as she slid on her sunglasses. "The one about me staying with you. I'm officially homeless in Kansas City and New York."

Hope turned her head toward him and removed the sunglasses she'd just put on. "You're homeless in New York?"

"Yeah. Funny, the landlord decided that it was my neglect that caused my apartment to get broken into. He sees that, as I trashed the place, he no longer wants me or Bryce as tenants of said space."

"Bryce?"

"My roommate."

"Wow, so he evicted you?"

"Yep. So up to the fourth floor I went to grovel to the redhead with the big boobs who's been chasing me for the past three months."

"Oh." She replaced her sunglasses and started the car. "So you're going to stay with her?"

"Didn't I just ask to stay with you?"

Hope turned to him, her brows knit behind the shield of her glasses. "Well... yes."

"Okay."

"So what's with the redhead?"

"Trying to see if it gets under your skin. That means you're into me." He slid his own sunglasses on and smiled.

"Trevor, that's not nice."

"What's nice is that Bryce has the hots for the redhead, who, I was told over and over again, has a name. Patricia, I think he said. But she took him in and all of his crap."

"Oh." She shook her head. "So he's living in the same building he was evicted from, with the redhead who has big boobs who was chasing you?"

"Yep that sums it up."

"And you're not living in New York anymore?"

"Doesn't look like it."

She hadn't moved the car. She didn't say anything else. He turned to her, pulled his sunglasses from his face, and adjusted himself in the seat.

"There isn't anywhere else in the world I'd rather be than right here with you." He watched her swallow hard. "Did I make a mistake?"

She shook her head and pulled her sunglasses off, again, and tears began to stream down her cheeks.

"Hope, don't be sad. I can make arrangements..."

"Don't you dare." She smiled as she sniffed back her tears. "My grandmother told me in a dream once you'd come searching for me, and here you are."

"Here I am."

"Did you come searching for me, Trevor?"

His heart kicked up a notch, and he pressed his palms against his thighs to keep his hands from shaking. "Yes. I did in fact come searching for you."

"Then that would explain why I've fallen in love with you." She smiled and raised her hand to his cheek. "I fell in love with you the moment I saw you," she whispered. "I only paint those I love."

Hope slid her sunglasses back on her face and backed out of the parking space.

"So how is your family?"

"Oh, fine. Mom looks forward to meeting you in a few weeks."

Hope smiled. "You told her about me?"

"I don't have to tell my mother much. She knows me pretty well. We're very close."

"So she knows I've stolen your heart."

"Yes," he said, reaching for her hand and interlacing their fingers. "Why don't you call your sister and have her meet us at your... our place when she's done teaching."

Hope nodded and dialed the phone while she sat at a stoplight. Trevor watched her carefully as she spoke to her sister. She didn't look toward him and she answered any questions that Carissa was asking with a grunt. Something had transpired while he'd been gone. He had his secrets, and now it seemed she had her own.

Hope pulled up in front of the apartment, and Trevor hurried to her side of the car to open her door.

Hope stepped out and rested a hand on his arm. "You know, I could really get used to that."

"You'll have to. I'll always be doing it." He leaned in and kissed her. "I guess you'll need to get used to me saying something else too."

"What's that?" she asked, her lashes fluttering up at him.

"That I love you."

"I love you too."

"Maybe after your sister leaves, we can have a nice long talk about us." He'd put it out there and even behind her sunglasses he knew her eyes had changed. "A fill-in-the-blanks kind of talk."

Hope nodded, then shut the door and started across the street.

Trevor carried his suitcase and the box from Ruth up the stairs and stood behind her as she slid the key into the lock, but she didn't have to turn it, the door pushed in.

"What in the…"

"Don't move." Trevor dropped his suitcase and the box.

He pushed open the door and stood for a moment. Reaching inside the door, he took an umbrella from her umbrella stand and gripped it in his hands like a weapon.

"Don't move," he whispered to her and she nodded.

He stepped into the hallway and looked down the hall toward the kitchen and back toward the living room. He took a few more steps and then stopped. The entire living room had been torn apart, the bookshelves emptied, and desk drawers pulled out. He walked down to the bedroom. It too had been gone through. Trevor backed his way through the kitchen. Cupboard doors were left open, and a few broken plates crunched under his foot, but there was no one in the apartment but him.

He walked back to the door and found a frightened Hope. Without the case he'd never have found her. But if

Donald Buchanan hadn't walked into his office perhaps she'd be safe.

He gritted his teeth and he felt the hard ball of anger form in his stomach. "They hit you. It's torn apart."

Chapter Nine

Hope didn't say a word as tears began to stream from beneath her sunglasses. What could be beyond the door? How much of her life was destroyed?

Trevor wrapped his hands around her arms and gave them a gentle rub. "Why don't we lock this up and call the police. I'll take you to your sister's house or your parents'."

She shook her head. "No. They may have scared Mandy away, but they aren't going to scare me away."

"What do you mean they scared Mandy away?"

Hope tucked her lips between her teeth, not yet ready to tell him what she'd learned of her birth mother. She pulled her sunglasses from her eyes, slid from Trevor's grip, and stepped into her apartment to see firsthand what Trevor had found.

"Oh damn!" She covered her mouth with her hand. The pictures of her family had been torn from the walls. Books had been dumped into the floor, and the cushions from the furniture discarded to the side of the room. She walked to her bedroom and stood at the doorway, afraid to walk in. The bed was turned over, the dresser drawers emptied, and the contents of her closet had been thrown throughout the room.

"You feel violated, don't you? Nothing like someone touching all your things."

She felt sick to her stomach. "Did they leave anything intact?"

"No. I'll call the police," he offered and she nodded. "Look around. Do you see anything missing?"

"How would I know?" she bit off quickly, then let out a heavy breath. "I'll look."

Trevor opened his cell phone and called the police while Hope carefully walked through the rubble that was her life.

She picked up a picture of her family taken at her high school graduation while Trevor explained to the police what had happened. She looked at the joy that beamed from her father's eyes and at Sophia who looked at her with such love. What was she doing? These were her parents. Why did she think she needed to hurt them to find out who she was?

Trevor closed his cell phone and walked over to her. He looked down at the picture in her hand and rested a hand on her shoulder. "They're on their way. Did you find anything missing?"

She shook her head. "No. They didn't find what they were looking for."

"Hope, what are they looking for?"

She didn't have a chance to answer before there was a gasp at the door. They both turned to see Carissa standing in the doorway.

"Oh, dear God! What happened in here?" She looked around. "They hit you too?"

"Looks that way." Hope walked around the cushions and scattered books back toward the door.

"Thank goodness you weren't here."

"They would have waited. I don't think they're looking to hurt any of us. They're looking for something." Hope focused on Carissa, who she knew would understand the meaning behind it.

Carissa nodded and turned to Trevor. "Hope said you brought something back with you."

"I did, but I think we should wait until the police leave to go through it."

She shifted her eyes back to Hope. "I think we should tell him."

Hope pursed her lips as she contemplated her sister's words. She hadn't wanted to tell him about the contents of the safety deposit box yet. She hadn't completely been able to grasp the truth around the letters, stocks, and money. Before she could say a word, Trevor stepped up to her.

"Tell me what?"

Carissa straightened her shoulders. "While you were in New York, we located the safe-deposit box."

"You did?" Amazement and then anger flashed in his eyes. "That could have been dangerous. Why would you do that?" He rubbed his hand over his forehead and took a deep breath. "Where did you find it?" he asked in a calmer tone.

"It was in a bank in Jefferson City," Carissa said.

Trevor narrowed his eyes. "How would you know to look that far away?"

"That's where I closed out the other accounts that she'd had twenty-three years ago. I didn't close out the box because I didn't know to ask about it." Carissa opened her purse and pulled out the stock certificates. She handed them to Trevor. "This is what was in there."

"The stocks." His eyes widened.

Hope studied him as he looked at them. There was a glimmer in his eye that spoke of more than just curiosity. She hated that fear flickered in her; Carissa may be right and he shouldn't be trusted. "The stocks? You sure say that like you knew something about them."

Trevor shifted his stance and thumbed through the papers in his hand. "I just found out about them. I didn't know they were in Mandy's possession."

Carissa narrowed her eyes on Trevor. "How exactly did you just find out about them?"

"Ruth." He fixed his eyes on hers.

"Ruth? You talked to Ruth?" Carissa's voice rose. "How did you get to her?"

"Wait." Hope walked closer to them, holding her hands with her palms out to stop them from continuing without her involved in the conversation. "Who is Ruth?"

Carissa let out a forced laugh. "Do you not tell her anything about who you're talking to?"

"I haven't had the chance yet," he argued, but Hope could hear the control it was taking to keep his voice calm.

"Hello? Who the hell is Ruth?" Hope asked again, her patience draining.

"The mother of the woman you think you need to find out about," Carissa snapped and walked to the kitchen.

Hope and Trevor followed her. She pulled a glass from the cupboard and filled it with water. Hope noticed her hands shake as she held the glass.

She picked up one of the kitchen chairs that lay on the floor, giving herself a moment to control the anger that was fighting its way to the surface. "Why do I feel completely left out of the loop? Why don't I know about Ruth?"

"Remember I told you she said never to contact her again?" Carissa reminded her.

"You told Hope you called Ruth?" Trevor asked.

Hope turned to Trevor and gritted her teeth. "You knew she'd talked to this woman?" Trevor nodded, and Hope wondered what else they had spoken about and neglected to tell her.

Carissa leaned against the counter and sipped her water. "Why did you go? Why did you find her?"

"I was close by. I figured it was worth a shot."

"And she didn't shoot you at the door?"

He smiled. "Oh, I think she might have wanted to, but I had information she didn't."

"Oh yeah? What could you have told her she didn't already know?" Carissa's tone was crass and Hope didn't like the way she was talking to him. She didn't like the fact that he knew more than she did either. And she didn't like that they had their own secret. She was growing very tired of all the secrets.

Trevor took a defensive step toward Carissa. "I told her that her daughter was dead," he said, and Carissa's shoulders dropped from their defensive position.

She rubbed the bridge of her nose and shook her head. "She didn't even know her own daughter was dead?"

"She said she remembered you calling. She knew she was nasty to you and she'd meant to be. She figured Mandy had put you up to calling and that she was after something. Then when Mandy died, she received a vague letter. It said she'd had another baby and died. Again, she figured someone was just trying to get money from her and that they'd been put up to it by Mandy."

Carissa shook her head. "It's sad that she could be so cold."

"I hate to tell you. She's really not that bad. She was a very warm woman."

It wouldn't have been what Hope would have expected someone to say about the woman who gave birth to Mandy Marlow. She had assumed Mandy's callous ways came from the people who raised her.

"She's the one who sent me the box for you both," Trevor offered.

"Mandy's mother?" Hope finally spoke. Trevor nodded. "Can we see it now?"

"We should probably wait until the police get here."

Hope didn't want to wait. She'd waited long enough, and the sincere pout on her face must have hit the right chord with Trevor. He picked up the box he'd brought with him from New York and set it on the kitchen table. Both Hope and Carissa picked up chairs, sat down at the table, and stared at the box.

They exchanged uneasy glances before Carissa finally lifted the lid and looked inside.

Her eyes were misty and open wide as she looked inside. "You must have done a lot of talking to her."

"I did. That's why she gave you the box." He leaned forward. "She didn't want you to know only the woman you have in your mind. She wanted you to know the daughter she once had. The girl who sat on her daddy's lap and swam in lakes. The girl who was an artist and won ribbons for her work."

Hope smiled. She felt as though a piece of her that had been missing was replaced.

"Does she want to meet us?" she asked.

Trevor shook his head. "No."

"Oh," Hope said and her shoulders dropped. "I thought…"

"Things might change," he added. "For now she's afraid that Mandy caused you enough harm that knowing her would only be a bad thing. She knows you grew up in a loving home, and for that she's happy. She's not willing to step on the toes of your family."

"Well it seems she's not the witch I thought she was," Carissa said, lifting out the ribbon that lay in the box. "I guess you know where you got your art talent from." She handed the ribbon to Hope.

"First place." She turned the ribbon over. "Presented to Mandy Marlow for her portrait of a sunset." She swallowed hard and looked up at Trevor. "Thank you for this."

"You're welcome."

The girls continued through the box and Trevor made a pot of coffee, careful not to disturb the mess around them or any evidence the intruder might have left behind. As it brewed, the doorbell rang. He hurried to the door assuming the police had finally arrived, but he was surprised to find David there, his brow furrowed.

"I want to talk to you," he said, passing by him, Trevor felt a knot in his stomach. He was already battling with the guilt of hiding information from Hope and sharing too much information with Carissa. Now David Kendal wanted to talk to him, and he wasn't feeling good about it.

David walked toward the kitchen and saw his daughters poring over the box of memorabilia. He looked around the room. "Jesus Christ! What happened?"

Hope stood from the table. "Dad, someone broke in. No one is hurt. Nothing is missing. We're waiting for the police."

"Waiting for the police? You shouldn't be in here!" His temple twitched and Trevor wished Hope would let him take her away before the police arrived. David turned to face him and Trevor straightened his shoulders. "You let her stay here? What are you thinking?"

"She wanted to stay."

"She's not thinking clearly, obviously."

"Dad." Hope stepped between her father and Trevor. "He offered. I wanted to stay."

David let out a long breath and then nodded toward the table. "What is that?"

Carissa sat up taller and focused her eyes on her father's. "It's a box of pictures and items from Mandy's childhood."

David turned his disapproving glare back toward Trevor, and the knot in his stomach tightened, almost forcing him to take a seat, but he stood where he was and tried to keep his eyes steady.

"Hope said your hotel room was broken into."

"It was."

"And your home and your office?"

Trevor swallowed hard. "Yes."

"And now this." He let his eyes settle on the mess surrounding them. "Do you have any idea who's behind this?"

"I have some ideas, but no. I don't know who exactly."

Carissa laid down the pictures, opening her mouth, but David turned his stare toward Hope. "Who is the woman who came into your store today? She came looking for you. Red lipstick, black purse, and looking mean as hell."

"I don't know." Hope walked to stand by Trevor. He reached for her hand and gave it a squeeze, hoping to ease the pain he could see in her eyes, brought on by his angering her father. "She came in a few days ago and looked around. She said she was going to come back. She gave me the creeps."

"Well she knew me. As she put it, I was the 'first one Mandy Marlow sunk her claws into.'"

The knot in Trevor's stomach moved into his chest. His breath caught in his lungs and his mouth went dry.

"Delores Buchanan." He let out a loud breath, and all eyes turned toward him. He hadn't realized he'd spoken aloud until Hope's hand touched his arm and David's eyes grew narrow.

"Run that by me one more time," David said, his words slow and drawn out. Trevor suddenly feared the man he knew to be so calm.

"Delores Buchanan," Trevor repeated slowly.

"Donald Buchanan's wife?"

Trevor nodded.

"Why is Donald Buchanan's wife looking for my daughter?" David asked, but Trevor didn't have to answer. David's narrow stare changed, and his eyes opened wide as he backed himself to the chair behind him. "Oh—my—God!" He mashed his fist against his mouth and stared at Hope.

"What's going on? What am I missing?" Hope looked at her father and then at Trevor. "Who are Delores and Donald Buchanan?"

Trevor was unsure if he should speak. He could see David processing the information and scanning his eyes over Hope. David looked at him, and Trevor knew what he was silently asking. Trevor nodded, and David blew out a breath.

"I'm guessing that Donald Buchanan is your birth father," David answered.

"You know who my biological father is?" Her eyes were bright and hopeful, but he was sure that was going to change rather quickly.

"He had to be a good twenty years older than she was," David said. "Why would she have..." He stopped and looked up at Trevor. "Her father's company. She was after the money from her father's company."

"What does this Buchanan have to do with Mandy?" Carissa finally asked her father.

"Donald Buchanan was the partner of Curtis Marlow. They owned a medical supply company. They used the charter airline company that I worked for when I first started flying. We did flights for them six and seven times a week."

"If they were flying chartered jets they had to be making some pretty good money," Carissa added.

"They were. As far as I knew. I didn't work for the company very long, but long enough to know who the Marlows and Buchanans were."

"So what happened to Curtis Marlow?"

"He died twenty-four years ago," Trevor said. "Ruth said that Donald was at his funeral, but Delores didn't attend. She did mention that she thought, after finding out he was your father, that maybe Mandy had sought out Donald to get Curtis's share of the company."

"What about the stocks?" Carissa asked.

"What stocks?" David turned to his older daughter. A crease formed between his brows.

Carissa shot glances at Hope and then to Trevor before standing and looking at her father. "Mandy had a safe-deposit box key on her key chain. Hope and I went to the bank in Jefferson City to see if she had a box there and she did."

"I thought you closed out everything when you turned eighteen." Anger filled his voice and Trevor's instinct was to pull Hope behind him to protect her, but he knew better.

Carissa shook her head. "I thought I did. I didn't know about the box. Hope found the key when she pulled out the box of things she had that belonged to Mandy."

David nodded. "What are the stocks?"

"They were in the box." Carissa shrugged.

Figuring most of the information had already been presented, Trevor added what he knew. "Ruth Marlow said that after her husband died, Donald Buchanan bought her shares of the company from her. It was the last she'd thought about it, but about a month ago, Delores Buchanan approached her about them."

Carissa shook her head. "Wait. Twenty-four years after Curtis Marlow dies and Donald Buchanan buys his partner's widow's shares of the company, the wife comes looking for them?"

Trevor nodded.

"So where is Buchanan through all of this?" Carissa asked.

Trevor couldn't help his instinct to look at Hope when he said, "He's recovering from a massive heart attack and bypass surgery."

Her reaction was what he'd feared. She bit her lip when it started to quiver and her eyes and welled up with tears. She turned her head so that David didn't see, but Trevor saw.

"What doesn't make sense to me is if he's lying in a hospital recovering from massive surgery, what is she doing here looking for Hope?"

Carissa sighed. "There was a letter."

"A letter? What letter?" David watched as Hope opened her purse and pulled out the letter they had found in the box. She handed it to David and watched him scan the envelope before pulling out the contents.

David read over it, took a deep breath, and handed it to Trevor. "Did you know about this?" he asked him and Trevor shook his head. "So Mandy has an affair with Donald Buchanan. He gives her her father's part of the company in stocks. She doesn't tell him she's pregnant, and the wife pays her off to disappear."

Carissa nodded. "Sounds like it."

"Where's the money?"

Carissa closed her eyes and winced. "It was there." She stood to face her father. "When you gave me power of attorney I closed out the account. Dad, she had over a hundred grand in there."

"Excuse me?" His eyebrows rose and his mouth hung open.

Carissa nodded. "I took it. I was mad. I figured she owed it to me."

"And exactly what did you do with that kind of money?" His jaw tensed and the vein on the side of his neck pulsed.

This time she smiled. "I put myself through college. Something she never would have done for me."

"You said you wouldn't let us help you with that. You said you'd work for it."

"I lied," Carissa stated it simply. "Mandy covered the bills. I took the rest when I bought the building for the school and used it as the down payment."

"Your mother signed on that building with you."

"Yes. But she didn't know where the down payment came from. She only knew I'd been saving."

David continued to shake his head. "Well, at least you got something out of it." He pinched the bridge of his nose.

"There was ten thousand more in cash in the box," Carissa added. "My guess is that Delores Buchanan only recently found out that Mandy Marlow has been dead for twenty-three years and wants her money back."

Hope looked from person to person and she obviously struggled to put all the pieces together. "If she's after the stocks because she knows Mandy's gone and her husband is lying in some hospital bed, why did she start with Trevor?"

Hope's question made Trevor's throat close up. He nearly lost his balance, blindsided by her innocence.

He tried to keep his composure. He felt as if he was on a cliff and the edge was slipping out from under his feet. Hope needed to know Donald had hired him. There wasn't time for confidential client relations now that she'd been attacked.

As he took a breath to say whatever was going to come out, there was a tap at the open door. A police officer stood just beyond the doorway, another behind him.

"We're responding to a breaking-and-entering call."

An hour after the police officers arrived, they left with their notes. It was quite a coincidence that Trevor's hotel had been hit and so had Hope's apartment, the police had decided. They thought it would be best if Carissa and her family found a place to stay for a few days. There seemed to be a pattern and it could possibly be that they'd hit her home next. The officers promised that they would have a car pass by the house on an hourly basis.

David shut the door as the officers left. "Carissa, you call Thomas and have him pack up things for you and the kids. You and Hope head over to our house. Trevor and I are going to try and reassemble some of this."

Trevor felt the sickening effect of panic take over again. He kept reminding himself of what a sincere and gentle man he knew David Kendal to be, but as he watched Hope gather some clothes and toiletries, he began to wonder if he should just run for the door and not turn back. Did he really want to be alone with her father in such a situation?

No, he didn't.

Hope was the one who brought up the subject that they'd broken into his place. He'd almost had to answer for his actions, and now he'd be alone with her father, whom he also noted was very bright. Surely David hadn't missed the fact that they had hit him first, second, and third before going after Hope.

Trevor carried Hope's bag out to Carissa's car and set it in the backseat.

"I guess I'll see you in just a little bit," Hope said rising up on her toes and kissing him.

"Did they happen to steal your kitchen knives? I wouldn't want any weapons in the house if I'm alone with your father."

She shook her head and smiled. "You forget who you're dealing with. David Kendal is the nicest, softest, and calmest man you'll ever meet."

"Right. I'm going to keep repeating those words to myself as I go back inside and hope that I come back out alive."

"I love you. That's reason enough for him to love you too."

"Yeah, well, I don't think your family shares your view. But I welcome the optimism."

Hope kissed him again. "Just be you. Everything is going to be okay."

He watched Carissa drive away. Hope waved. Then he turned his attention back to the apartment and slowly climbed the steps.

David picked up the turned-over furniture and stacked items he found on the floor on the coffee table.

"They did a fine job on this." He held up a broken picture frame, studied it, and then added it to a pile. "Maybe tomorrow you can help her sort through all this. I think half of it will have to be thrown away."

Trevor moved farther into the room and picked up a few items himself. He'd taken the word tomorrow to mean he'd be alive and with Hope the next day.

"I'll help her get this all put together and get the locks changed. It wouldn't hurt to have some security added to the windows too. I know a lot of people…" he stopped when he realized David was ready to speak.

"You know who did this and you know what they're looking for." It wasn't a question, Trevor quickly realized, and he had to hand it to David Kendal, he was straightforward.

He blew out a breath and gathered his courage. He laid the book he'd picked up from the floor on the end table. "I think I know who."

"Delores Buchanan?"

"I don't think she did this personally, but I'm sure she has people."

David nodded, considering. "She knew who I was. I had no idea who she was. I don't remember her at all. But then again I was twenty-two years old. I wasn't paying attention to executive's wives." David picked up another frame and added it to the pile. "Isn't it funny. I don't think I ever thought to ask Mandy who Hope's father was."

"You're her father," he reminded him.

David smiled. "Yes, I am. That was the hardest and best decision I ever made. I was sure I would lose Sophia over it, but I could never have turned away Carissa's blood." He cleared a place and sat on the sofa. With weary eyes, he looked around and then leaned forward, his elbows on his knees, and his hands clasped together.

"Did Donald send you to find Hope?"

Trevor moved and sat in the chair closest to him. If it had been that obvious, why hadn't Hope asked him the same question?

Trevor cleared his throat. "A month ago he walked into my office. He set down half my fee on my desk, in cash, for finding a missing person. He was looking for Mandy Marlow and he hadn't the first idea how to find her. It was just a case to me."

He leaned back in the chair and raked his fingers through his hair. Though David was looking at his own hands, Trevor took solace in the fact that he was calm so he continued. "Ruth Marlow wasn't any help. No one in New

York seemed to know who she was. It took me two weeks to track down something solid. The solid lead was you."

"Me?"

Trevor nodded. "Any records I could find of her were attached to you. You're on Carissa's birth certificate. Her last known address is your address. That's when I began to look into Mandy Kendal."

David sat back and scrubbed his hands over his face. "She always knew how to get to me."

"It's not really that hard to change your name anymore. Legally or illegally," he assured him.

"So you know I never married her?"

"I know." Trevor thought he looked grateful that someone believed him.

"After all these years, why did he want to find Mandy?"

"It seems he came into the knowledge that there was a child."

"He didn't know? For twenty-three years he had no idea?"

"That's what I understand. So my job was to find Mandy Marlow and see if she had a child about twenty-three years old."

"He must not have been too interested in meeting her."

"I think he was in shock when he found out that Mandy was dead."

"He didn't know that?"

"No. He's only ever asked me Hope's first name. But he sent me more money and asked me to get to know her. The time wasn't right for him to meet her and he was afraid of his wife. She wasn't to know about Hope or about me looking for Mandy."

The depth of color in David's cheeks deepened. He squeezed together his fingers until his knuckles were white.

David's Adam's apple bobbed slowly, and Trevor readied himself.

"You've moved in on my daughter because Donald Buchanan paid you to do so?" he asked through clenched teeth.

"I approached your daughter because he asked me to."

"She's under the impression that you two have some kind of future together. But she's 'just another case?'"

"No, it's not like that."

"Really, it sounds like that's exactly what it is." David stood and Trevor followed, bracing for his shift in attitude.

He tried to swallow the lump of fear that had lodged itself in his throat. It wasn't going down easily. "Sir, I've been in love with your daughter for a very long time."

David's eyes narrowed and Trevor moved behind the chair and gripped the back of it for support.

"This is going to sound very stupid to a man as smart as you. But I've seen her in my dreams. It was as if I was looking for this perfect woman all along and then there she was. I do love your daughter, and I don't ever want to see her hurt."

"You expect me to believe that this is all okay because you've dreamed about her?"

"And she's dreamed about me too." He raked his fingers through his hair again.

Every word he spoke made him sound like a complete idiot. But he couldn't stop himself. He just had to keep talking.

"I know this is all very sudden and I don't seem like the ideal man for her."

"You're a mind reader too," David spat out.

"But I hope you can see past the circumstances and know that I truly care about your daughter."

David paced the room. The color in his cheeks had returned to normal and Trevor was relieved by that, though he still kept his distance from David and blocked his entrance to the kitchen with his body.

"I may be an over-protective father, but I am a man. I fell in love once too. Hard and quick." He sat back down on the sofa and smiled ruefully. "Mr. Investigator, did you know I proposed to my wife the first time we went out?"

"No."

"I proposed to her for years. It took thirteen for us to finally get married. But I knew I loved her and always would. I never gave up on that, even though she did for a bit."

"When she played for Pablo DiAngelo?"

David nodded. "You've done your homework. I'm not sure I'm comfortable with that." Trevor tensed, but relaxed a bit as David turned and faced the windows. "She wanted children and couldn't have them. When I agreed to take Hope I thought it would be her chance to have a baby, but I knew just how stupid it sounded."

He stared out the window for a moment. "She wasn't an easy sell, but when she realized what I was willing to lose to keep Carissa and her sister together, she knew it was our opportunity to have a family. She's never thought of Hope as anyone else's but her own."

"Hope loves Sophia. She loves you both."

"That's why I don't want to see her hurt. If Delores Buchanan wants those stocks, back then I say we hand the damn things over. This has gone too far."

"You seem to be the only person who has talked to her. I can't get her to answer her phone. She left her husband in the hospital."

"Do you think she'll hit Carissa's house?"

"It's completely possible. Especially if she knows they drove all the way to Jefferson City to a bank."

David nodded. "Maybe you should get Hope out of town for a few days."

Trevor thought it a good sign that David would consider him being with Hope again. "I asked her to go to New York with me to meet my mother. I want to give her the painting Hope did as a gift."

Again, relief flooded him when David smiled. "She's quite an artist, isn't she?"

"I think so."

"Can you make the trip earlier? I don't want her here, where we know Delores Buchanan is."

"We can leave tomorrow morning."

"Okay. She's staying with us tonight."

Trevor nodded. "I'll pick her up in the morning, then. I'll make arrangements tonight."

"Thank you for being a gentleman about it," David said as he walked toward him and then patted him on the back. "I'd love to have you stay, but…"

"I wouldn't even dream of it."

Chapter Ten

Hope settled into bed with her nieces on either side of her. She'd hoped Trevor would stay with her parents too, but he'd called and explained that he felt more comfortable at a hotel. She couldn't blame him, but when they went to New York to visit his parents he'd better not suggest she go to a hotel.

He'd told her the plans to take her to New York the next morning. When she'd voiced her concern, her father had laid his hand on her shoulder and comforted her.

"It's best for you to go now. We'll watch the store and take care of your apartment. Besides, the man who loves you wants to show you off," he'd said with a smile, then leaned in closer to her. "He'll also protect you if anything happens."

Julie rolled over, pulling the blankets with her and uncovering her sister. Becky, sound asleep, wiggled closer to Hope for warmth. Hope chuckled quietly and adjusted the blankets over all of them. It would prove to be an interesting night, she thought. She closed her eyes and quickly drifted to sleep.

Since she'd met Trevor, he hadn't filled her dreams. He was her reality now. But tonight she dreamed of him. She swam in and out of sleep, tossing and turning as she tried to shake the image of him standing with Delores Buchanan, laughing at her. She told herself she loved him, but there were so many things that didn't line up quite right.

No matter how hard she tried, she couldn't wake up, and he continued to laugh at her.

"Hope, be careful." Katie's voice broke through Trevor's laughter.

"I am careful, Grandma," Hope said. She rested her head on her grandmother's shoulder, their hands clasped together as they walked through clouds.

"He's here to protect you and love you. But things don't seem to be going smoothly."

"Oh, Grandma, you worry too much."

"That's my job. I'm supposed to worry about you. I didn't get to spend enough time with you. I only want you happy like your mother and your sister are."

"I am happy." Hope stopped and looked at her grandmother, whose face shimmered and glowed. "I love Trevor. I want to marry him."

Katie nodded and smiled. "Be careful, Hope," she said again before she faded away.

The girls were gone when Hope awoke. The room had filled with sunlight and she rubbed the sleep from her eyes, trying to wake fully.

"Good morning, sleepyhead," her mother said as she opened the door to her childhood room.

"What time is it?"

"Nine thirty."

Hope sat straight up and ran her fingers through her hair. "I guess yesterday took more out of me than I thought. That or sleeping with those girls." She shook her head, thinking about the war that had continued throughout the night with legs and arms flailing.

"They adore you."

"I love them so much. It's funny to think I was my nephew's age when he was born. I've been an auntie half my life."

Sophia walked into the room and sat down on the bed. She rested her hand on Hope's leg over the covers.

"Your father had a lot to say about Trevor."

Hope winced and then let out a sigh. "He doesn't like him, does he?"

"On the contrary, he only had nice things to say about him."

"Really?" She was completely shocked and it resonated in her voice.

"Why do you seem so surprised?"

"Because it's only been a few weeks since we met. Because most of the time I've spent with him has revolved around Mandy." She dropped her shoulders. "Because when I asked him to help me find out more about my birth parents, it hurt you." Hope reached for Sophia's hand and held it. "I'm still very sorry about that."

Sophia smiled. "You never would have made that decision if you thought it would hurt me. I'll admit my feelings were hurt. But that's all. You deserve to know everything you can. They can't take you away from me now."

"They never could have, Mom. You are my mother. You're the only mother I know."

Sophia raised her hand to Hope's cheek and caressed it as she had when she was a child. "I'm glad I didn't walk away when your father chose to keep you. Now you're all grown up and it looks like you've fallen in love too."

"I have."

Sophia nodded and replaced her hand within Hope's. "I'm your mother. I'm supposed to tell you to be careful."

"Grandma already told me."

Sophia opened her mouth to speak and reconsidered. "You're dreaming about her again?"

"Yes."

Sophia shook her head. "Leave it to my grandmother to still meddle in people's lives thirteen years after she died."

"Do you believe in things like that?" Hope asked, already knowing the answer.

"My parents used to come to me in dreams. It gave me comfort to think they were still with me after they died. I felt like they watched me grow up."

"I miss her."

"I do too." Sophia blew out a breath, and Hope watched as she batted away a tear. "Well, you'd better get some things together. That man that makes your eyes sparkle will be here in an hour to take you to meet his mother."

Hope felt the blood drain from her face. "I'm scared to death."

"Don't be," Sophia laughed. "She will love you."

"Do you really think so?"

She patted her hand. "I know so."

Trevor rang the doorbell after having stood on the front porch of the house for almost five minutes collecting his thoughts. He heard the young voice announce that she'd answer the door moments before it flung open.

"Hi, Mr. Jacobs."

"Good morning…" He stopped, unable to remember her name.

"Julie. I'm Julie."

"Good morning, Julie," he said realizing that she was the one who resembled Mandy so closely. "Is your aunt here?"

"Yeah, she's here." She ran toward the back of the house, and Trevor shut the front door.

Hope appeared a moment later and smiled just as she had in his dream the night before.

"You look beautiful," he said as he crossed to her and kissed her gently on the lips. They were soft. It was a welcome warmth after he'd lost hours of sleep worrying about her.

"I missed you last night," she whispered as she ran her hands up his chest and he wrapped his arms around her waist. After yesterday, to have her embrace him settled his nerves. Perhaps she hadn't realized just how deep into the investigation he was on both sides.

"How could you miss me? You had your entire family hovering over you."

"I slept with six- and eight-year-old cover hogs."

Trevor smiled. "That must be where you get it."

Hope's eyes opened wide and she shook her head. "Beware, Mr. Jacobs." She drew her eyebrows together. "Insult me again and you may be sleeping alone for a very long time."

He laughed as she turned, grabbed his hand, and pulled him to the small kitchen where her family sat crowded around the table.

"Good morning, Trevor." Sophia greeted him with a cup of coffee.

"Good morning."

David stood and silently shook his hand. They had a pact. David knew all his secrets. With one word, he could make or break Trevor's relationship with Hope.

Trevor sat down with her family while Hope finished the last of her packing. They talked with him and around him as though he were a part of their day-to-day life. They did it all without one word about Mandy Marlow, break-ins, or company stocks. He noticed David never looked up from his newspaper and he was okay with that. He didn't know if he could carry on a nonchalant conversation with the man yet. He was, however, eternally grateful that David hadn't told anyone about his connection to Donald Buchanan. If he had, Trevor assumed he wouldn't be sitting calmly among them. Sophia would have been frying him up on the stove instead.

"So when you get back to Kansas City will you set up shop for yourself?" Carissa asked. "Hope told me you wouldn't be staying in New York any longer."

His eyes widened. She obviously trusted them with almost everything. A shiver ran through him. Just how much about their relationship had Hope shared with her family?

"Um, yeah. My mom has connections everywhere. So I'll sit down with her this week and brainstorm on a plan. I'd like to remain independent if I can."

"It's always nice to work for yourself," Thomas added.

"I've always enjoyed it." Trevor looked up as Hope walked through the doorway. "Are you all set?"

"I think so."

He stood and pushed in his chair. "Thank you for the coffee."

"Take care of our little girl," David said. He lowered his head and shot Trevor a look of warning before he kissed Hope on the cheek. "We'll take care of the shop and I'll keep an eye on the apartment too. You just try to relax and enjoy yourself."

"I will. I love you all."

They turned and walked out of the house. Trevor carried her suitcase, but before she could hurry away from him, he grabbed hold of her hand and interlaced their fingers.

"I was thinking. We really should ship the painting. I don't think it'll travel very well on the plane," Hope said as Trevor loaded her suitcase into the trunk on her car.

"That makes sense." He shut the trunk and before he opened her door, he pulled her to him hard, crushing his mouth to hers.

He'd missed the taste of her and the feel of her in his arms. It seemed like it had been weeks, when it had only been days.

"I missed you," he said with a whisper on her lips.

"I missed you too."

Hope was quiet during the flight. Her nerves twisted her gut.

Trevor took her hand. "Nervous?"

"Extremely."

"My folks are great. I don't want you to worry. They are going to love you."

She let out a sigh. "I believe you. But Trev"—she turned in her seat toward him as the plane landed—"I've been thinking. Since we're in New York... I want to meet Donald Buchanan."

Trevor's lips pursed and he looked out the window as the plane taxied to the terminal. "With everything going on with his wife, I don't know if that's a good idea. I mean, I promised your family that I would keep you safe and away from harm."

Hope nodded. She wouldn't pursue it further. At least not with him.

The tension of meeting his mother was quickly dealt with when Hope and Trevor walked around the wall to the baggage claim, and there stood his parents waiting for him. Hope would have known his father anywhere. He was simply a version of Trevor with an additional twenty-five years on him. Violet Jacobs stood prim and proper, dressed immaculately with pearls and pumps. The smile on her face was that of a woman who had missed her son, even if she'd only seen him off the day before.

"Trevor, I was so glad you called." She wrapped her arms around his neck and planted a loud kiss on his cheek. "I know I fed you breakfast yesterday, but knowing you were moving away, I missed you bunches since then."

"Mom, you're so sappy."

"Always have been, always will be." She smiled as she patted him on the cheek and then her smile turned to Hope. "You must be Hope." She extended her perfectly manicured hand toward her and shook Hope's trembling one. "Trevor spent the better part of his last visit talking about you. It is so nice to finally meet you."

"It's nice to meet you too, Mrs. Jacobs."

"Oh, there will be none of that." Violet patted her hand. "I am Violet. And this quiet beast here is Brandon."

Brandon took a step forward and shook her hand.

"Glad to meet you." He glanced at Trevor. "Didn't think you'd come back so soon. I figured I would have to take more of Bryce's money before I got to take more of yours."

"Keep thinking that. Keep thinking it."

They walked to the parking garage, and Hope sat in the back seat with Violet. She could feel her eyes on her and she wanted to speak, but nothing would come out. The woman was as nice as could be, but Hope couldn't help but feel inferior looking at Violet's clothing, manicure, and hearing the precise tone in her voice, which demanded a respect. What would it be like, she wondered, to command the attention around you just by showing confidence?

Violet shifted in her seat to face Hope. "Hope, Trevor tells me you're an artist."

"Yes. I have a small gift shop where I sell my work." The smile was natural when she spoke of her store. She'd always figured it was like her child. She'd conceived it, nurtured it, and took very good care of it. Pride swelled inside her when someone asked about it.

"Oh, I think that is wonderful. I can't wait to see it. Tell me about your family."

Hope swallowed the lump in her throat and relaxed against the seat. "Well, my father is a retired airline pilot and my mother was a professional cellist before I was born. My sister and her husband run a music school."

Violet leaned forward and placed a hand on Trevor's shoulder. "Trev, you told me about her mom, right? She played in Europe?"

He nodded. "Yes, I told you that."

Hope smiled. "She and my brother-in-law toured with Pablo DiAngelo."

"That's right!" Violet wiggled in her seat. "Oh, he was one sexy man. I suppose he still is, but you don't hear about him much. Does your mother still keep in touch with him?"

"Christmas cards and they exchange e-mails. I've met him a few times, but that's really about it. To me he was just my mother's friend. I never thought of him as much more than that."

Violet nodded. "It sounds like your family is close knit, from what Trev tells me."

"We are." In all of her life she'd never known a family bound by blood that was closer than her own. "We are very close."

"I'm glad Trevor will have a family around. We'll miss him, but I know he'll be well taken care of."

Hope let out a silent breath as she relaxed around the woman who had been first and foremost in Trevor's life.

Violet tapped her fingertips together. "You know that landlord of yours dropped off a bill to the office, Trevor."

"A bill?" He turned in his seat until he was facing his mother, his arm flung over the back of the chair. "I took care of the damage to the apartment."

"Seems as though Scary Buchanan thinks you're hiding something."

Hope touched Trevor's arm. "I thought she was in Kansas City. That's why we came early." Her voice filled with panic.

"You're safe enough. We won't let anything happen to you," Violet assured her. "But Trevor, whoever broke into your apartment came back about the time you boarded the plane yesterday. They broke into your landlord's apartment, stole the keys, and hit that pretty redhead Bryce is staying with."

"Damn." Trevor pulled out his cell phone and dialed.

Hope sat back in her seat. Her quest to find out about her mother's past and the identity of her birth father was putting people in danger. But she'd come this far. She didn't think she could stop now.

Hope and Trevor settled into his old room. She was pleased to find that his parents were a little more open to their sharing a room.

Trevor opened the door to the bathroom.

"It joins the other bedroom, but there's no one in there. It used to be my sister's room."

"You had to share a bathroom with your sister?"

"Torture, right? Imagine an eight-year-old boy and a twelve-year-old girl. It was a good thing I didn't think hygiene was important yet. Her crap was all over all the time. I used to sit in there and spray everything. Sometimes I'd empty the container just to see how long it would take. Talk about pissing someone off."

"Not to mention the mess."

"Well since I always had to clean it up I wasn't going to mention it." He walked to her and wrapped his arms around her waist. "You look beat."

"It's been a busy few days."

"Tell you what." He kissed her gently. "You take a rest. My mom hasn't said anything, but I will guarantee you that by six o'clock this place is going to be packed. My guess is that my sister and her family and my ex-roommate, Bryce, will be here for dinner. Everyone wants to meet the woman who turned my life upside down."

Hope forced a smile. She was sure his ex-roommate and the redhead were going to be glad to meet her—after all, it was her fault Bryce had been kicked out of his apartment and the new one they shared had been broken into. She was bad luck. It was just a matter of time before someone made Trevor realize it.

David sat at Carissa's kitchen table and watched as his grandchildren ran out the back door and out into the yard where he'd married Sophia, and Carissa had married Thomas. Would his Hope be married in that yard? And would she be marrying Trevor?

When Thomas walked into the kitchen with a notepad, David gave him a nod and asked Carissa to sit with them.

"Now that Trevor has your sister out of the picture for a few days, Thomas and I thought we'd try to nab Buchanan's wife."

"Nab her? Like put her in a potato sack and throw her in the Missouri?" Carissa shook her hair over her shoulders and looked skeptically at him.

"Smart-ass. She wants to get to Hope. She wants those stocks and that money. I think she's the one behind all the break-ins."

"Well, not personally," Thomas added.

"Of course, but what are you going to do, Batman and Robin? How will you save us all?" Carissa's lips curled into a smile.

"I'm thinking we are going to use you for bait." David stated his plan and watched as her eyes went from humored to angry in a flash.

"Bait? Me?" Carissa turned to Thomas. "You're going to set me up?"

"She'll follow you if she knows Hope is gone."

"Neither of those things are settling well with me at this moment. I don't want to be bait and I don't like that Hope isn't with us."

"She's safe," David assured her.

"I think you threw her to the wolves."

"Carissa." Thomas reached for her hand. "Your father and I think this Buchanan woman knows you went to the bank and closed out the box. I did some searching and found that Donald Buchanan gave those stocks to Mandy. They are in her name. As it sits, you are the rightful owner of them as you have the power of attorney."

"I don't want it."

"Too late."

"I don't see why even from the grave Mandy Marlow sees fit to meddle in my life." She shoved back her chair and got up to pace a circle in the kitchen.

David stood and walked to Carissa. He held her arms and looked at her. After all the years they'd had together, he still couldn't see Mandy in her. She was his daughter through and through. "Listen. I won't let anything happen to you, and it should be fairly easy to get her in our grasp. But we need you to lead her to us."

He watched her mull it over.

She looked at Thomas, who nodded his head. Then she looked back at her father and narrowed her eyes.

Carissa sat back down at the table and David followed. She gripped her hands together and lifted her head. "What do I have to do?"

"You have to let them break into the house," David said.

"What? I'm not going to let that happen and put my children in danger." She turned to Thomas. "What if they hit the school? That puts our students in danger."

"Do you really think I'd do this if I thought it would danger our children?"

Carissa squeezed her eyes shut for a few seconds and let her shoulders drop before looking back at her husband. "No."

"Then listen to us for a minute," Thomas pleaded with her.

She shook her head. "I don't like this. I really don't like this." She huffed out a breath. "What do I need to do?"

David leaned his arms on the table. "We're going to do some surveillance on the house. Thomas has talked to the neighbors, and they're going to be keeping a keen eye on everything from front and back."

"Well, that shouldn't be hard. Mrs. Nelson watches everything that goes on from her window anyway. If you look out there right now you'll see the curtain move and her fingers poke through."

"She was old thirty years ago when I first started seeing your mother. There were a few occasions when she'd come out and yell at us for kissing in the moonlight." He smiled, he couldn't help himself. Those ten years Sophia disappeared from his life had all but been banished by the twenty-three years he'd had her as his wife.

"Back to them messing up my house."

"Well, we plan to catch them in the act. They seem to move during the day. We see them enter and we call the police."

"Dad, this sounds crazy. This isn't going to work."

"Let's try." He lifted his brows, and she nodded with a roll of her eyes. "Next, I went down to Hope's this morning and set up surveillance cameras at the store. If we can detain her long enough, we can get the police to her too."

"And charge her with what? Shopping in a gift store?"

"No, I think it will just be a matter of holding on to her for a few minutes until the police arrive. It's just a hunch that the goons she has busting up people's houses will squeal when in custody."

"Goons? Squeal? You've been watching too many cop shows."

"Maybe, but it's worth a try."

"I don't really care about the money or the stocks. We could just give them back to her."

David shook his head. "No. Donald Buchanan deserves the right to give them to his daughter if that's what he wants to do." It pained him to call Hope someone else's daughter. He'd never thought of her as anything but his own. After all, the very moment she was born, they'd handed her to him. He'd watched her take her first breath and witnessed every first from there on out. Just recently, he'd watched her fall in love, and, he thought, it looked good on her.

David let out a breath. "I don't think Donald has any ill will toward Mandy or Hope. After all, he sent Trevor to find her so he could meet her. I would assume he'd have her best interests at heart."

"He sent Trevor?" Carissa shot back up on her feet. "He was following her, wasn't he?"

"Yes, but—"

"But what? If she doesn't know that Trevor has been part of this from the start, then she's in more danger than we think. What is wrong with the two of you?"

Carissa headed to the phone on the wall and picked up the receiver. Thomas moved quickly and grabbed it from her hand. "What are you doing?"

"I think my baby sister needs to be warned she's with some lying, sleazy private investigator who is going to deliver her to Delores Buchanan on a silver plate."

"He's not doing that."

"You two are some piece of work. You let her go." She turned her angry eyes back to David. "You knew about this. How will I ever forgive you if something happens to her?"

Hadn't he lost sleep over that himself? If something happened to Hope, he'd never be able to live with himself. "Carissa, he isn't going to hurt her. He only wants what's best for her."

"I think you're crazy."

"Maybe." He stood and walked across the kitchen. "I can't help but believe that he loves her. I saw it in his eyes when he told me." He jammed his hands into his pockets. "Yes, Donald Buchanan hired him to find Mandy and to see if there was a child. Yes, he did his job. But in the meantime they fell in love."

"Carissa." Thomas's voice had her turning toward her husband. "You can't control when you fall in love, no matter how hard you fight not to."

She pursed her lips and shook her head. "I guess you would know."

"Exactly. Just trust us, okay? And trust that Trevor will do the right thing for Hope."

Carissa nodded and turned back to David. "And Hope is okay with this?"

David ran his hand over his hair. "Well, she doesn't know yet."

Carissa's eyes flew open and she yanked phone receiver back from Thomas's hands and began to dial her sister's number.

Thomas clamped his hand on the hook and cut off the call. "He'll tell her. If he loves her, he'll come clean. If she loves him, she'll understand." He took the phone from her hand and hung it back up. "Do you think so little of your sister?"

She scowled at him. "That's not fair."

"It's not fair that you won't give her a chance." He gathered her hands in his. "Let's do what we can from here. Let's try to stop these people who are ruining everyone's lives."

"And what happens when it falls apart? What happens when your bait and tackle doesn't work?"

"Then we offer back what they're after," David said. "Those pieces of paper mean nothing to us, and at least we know who's after them."

"If anything happens to her, I'm holding you two responsible."

"Fair enough."

"And the next time she calls, I'm asking her about Trevor. If he hasn't come clean, I'm telling her."

David didn't like it but he agreed.

She moved back to the table and picked up Thomas's notes. "Fine then. We need to find a place for the kids that they won't be touched. We need to cancel classes for a few days. Just tell the parents there's a water leak or something. And we need to get this over with and get her home." She turned back toward both of them, her hair flying over her shoulder. She lifted an unsteady hand and pointed at them. "If this goes bad, know that I'm not above killing him."

"Understood," David said, fearing it wasn't an idle threat.

"And I'll kill the two of you too if he hurts her."

"It won't come to that," he promised. God, let him be right.

Chapter Eleven

The mixing of voices woke Hope, and she stirred under the blanket atop Trevor's childhood bed. A calm filled her. He'd brought her home. She'd met his mother and his father.

She'd lain down for a few minutes and fallen asleep in the bed he'd fallen asleep in thousands of times.

The door creaked when it opened, and she turned her head to find Trevor standing there, the light at his back.

"Oh, good. You're awake." He moved into the room and sat on the edge of the bed next to her. He touched her cheek and ran his fingers back into her hair as she sat up to meet him. "I was right about dinner. Bryce and the redhead—"

"Her name is Patricia," she added, and he nodded.

"Right, Patricia. They're on their way over, and my sister and her family will be here in a half hour."

Hope sucked in a breath and ran her own fingers through her hair. Trevor watched her and she smiled, trying not to let on that she was completely a wreck of nerves. He lowered his forehead to hers.

"You don't have to be nervous around my family. My parents love you and the rest of them will too."

She already knew she liked his parents, but she also knew her being there had to cause her own parents heartache. Her mother had covered it well, but Hope knew Sophia didn't like the fact she still was on a quest to find out about her birth parents. And even though David encouraged them to take their trip earlier than planned, she couldn't help but notice the slightest bit of tension between him and Trevor when he'd picked her up at her parent's house. And then there was Carissa. Everything about Trevor unraveled her. What if his parents thought she was using him? What if his roommate and the redhead hated her for getting them caught in the crossfire of her desire to locate her birth father?

"I don't know when I've been this nervous." He pulled his head back and touched her cheek. "I love you. I've never felt about anyone else like I feel about you." He kissed the top of her head. "Take a few minutes and come on out."

Hope gave him a nod, and he walked out of the room.

The doorbell rang as Hope walked into the kitchen, where she found Trevor and his mother standing over a large pot at the stove. Violet held a glass of wine and Trevor a beer. She wondered what they were studying so closely.

"Hey, this guy brought a date. Did you tell him he could bring a date?" Brandon's voice carried through the house, and when Trevor turned to answer his father he noticed her in the doorway.

Warmth flickered in his eyes as he smiled. He walked to her, laid a kiss gently on her lips, and held her gaze as Bryce and his redhead walked through the door.

"Jesus, do you have to make out in the kitchen?"

Trevor kept her gaze. "Yep."

"Well at least let me get a look at her, man."

Trevor took a step back and Hope looked up at Bryce, who looked like he could be Trevor's brother. She decided that was a tribute to a long friendship.

He smiled and held out his hand. "I'm Bryce. I'm his better half."

"I thought that was me," she said coolly. "I'm Hope."

"Witty one. I like you." The woman to his side poked her elbow into his arm. "Oh, this is my roommate, Patricia."

Hope extended her hand and smiled politely, trying not to conjure up past conversations about the big-chested redhead. "Patricia, it's very nice to meet you."

"Likewise." She turned her stare to Trevor. The air had grown thick. "Nice to see you again."

The sound of children's laughter pealed from the front door. A little boy ran into the kitchen and right to Violet's leg. She scooped him up and planted noisy kisses on his face. Following him was a girl who looked about eight. Presumably this would be the girl he'd inquired about music lessons for.

A man entered next, his arms full of backpacks and in his hand a sippy cup, which he handed to the little boy in his grandmother's arms.

Finally, a very pregnant woman who must be Trevor's sister waddled into the crowded kitchen with their father following close behind. She rested her hands on her back and watched as the little boy squirmed out of Grandma's arms and toward her.

"He hasn't figured out I can't pick him up anymore." She tried to soothe him by patting his head, but in the end managed to squat down and pick him up.

"Taylor, you're the size of a house," Bryce blurted out, and both her husband and Brandon tried to conceal their snickers.

"And, Bryce, you're still a horse's ass." Her retort had Hope laughing, and Taylor's eyes shifted to her. "You must be Hope. I've heard so much about you." She walked toward her, the little boy still in her arms, and extended her hand. "I'm so glad you've come to meet us."

"Thank you. You have a beautiful family."

"Thanks. Let me introduce you. This is Collin, the little one over there is Sarah, and this is my husband Tim."

Tim stepped between them and shook Hope's hand before taking Collin from Taylor.

She rubbed her stomach. "This one is lovingly referred to as Elmo by Collin. And I know my mother's ears have perked up because she thinks I'll slip and tell her what the sex of the baby is."

"You are rotten," Violet called from over the pot on the stove, "and I have half a mind not to let you have any of these ribs that your father grilled. Trevor, come here, please. I didn't use quite enough…" She took his beer bottle and poured its contents into the pot.

The threat proved false, and soon Hope sat among the family she'd just met and felt at home. She figured this was how it was supposed to be if you were in love with someone. The entire family should be just as charming as the man who stole your heart away.

With his mouth full of ribs, Bryce said, "You're coming in to the office tomorrow, aren't you?"

Violet smacked him on the back of the head. "Not with your mouth full."

Taylor laughed aloud and Hope thought it amusing how Bryce fit like a member of the family. That was how she and Carissa were. They were a patchwork quilt as far as families went, but what they shared made them closer than some families who all shared blood.

Bryce finished his bite and washed it down with beer. "So you comin' or what? If you're really moving your butt to Kansas City, then I want your desk and the window. And the clients," he added, pointing his beer toward Trevor.

"Whatever you want, man."

Taylor sat back in her chair and pushed away her plate. "I can't believe you're moving."

"There's nowhere I'd rather be." He took Hope's hand and interlaced their fingers. "How can you argue with love?"

"You can when you're in labor," Taylor joked. "You couldn't pay me to move again."

Hope shifted her head and watched Taylor rub her stomach. Hadn't Trevor said she was moving? Hope and Thomas were both under the impression, as was her family, that his sister was moving to Kansas City too. Well, it must have been a miscommunication.

She washed up before bed and was slathering her skin with lotion when Trevor walked up behind her and wrapped his arms around her and nibbled her arm.

"You smell so good."

She only smiled.

"So." He stepped to the side of her in the bathroom and took out his toothbrush. "Tomorrow I'm going into the city with Bryce to go through the office. Mom's going in with us, so we'll leave her car for you. Feel free to go shopping or look around. Don't try to come into the city with the car though. We'll go in for dinner tomorrow so you can see it."

She nodded as he set his toothbrush down on the counter. He laid his hand gently on her arm and moved in closer to her. "Are you okay?"

"I'm fine. Sorry, just tired, I suppose."

"Well maybe this will be a restful weekend for you."

She wasn't sure about that. Since Taylor's comment about moving, she'd been replaying the past few weeks in her head. Who was the man she shared her bed with? She would have thought that being in New York, he would have mentioned something about her seeing Donald Buchanan or Ruth Marlow, but he hadn't. In fact, nothing had been said about it at all.

"I was thinking." He wrapped his arms around her and pulled her closer. "I've never had a girl sleep in my room before. In fact, I've never had a girl in my room before."

"You're mother doesn't seem like the kind of woman who would tolerate that."

"You've figured Violet Jacobs out very quickly." He traced a finger over her jaw. "You'll be the first girl I got tangled in the sheets with in my own bedroom."

Hope swallowed back the worry that was plaguing her and lifted a hand to Trevor's chest. "Maybe we'll try that some other time. The last thing I want is to upset your mother."

Disappointment slid over his face as he took a step back from her, his hands resting on her hips. "I didn't think being turned down would hurt. But ouch." He moved in and brushed a kiss over her lips. "Well then, I think I'll let you settle into bed and get some sleep. I, on the other hand, am going to sneak down to the kitchen and try to find those cookies my mother hides from the rest of the family."

Hope watched as he shut the door behind him. Trevor was hiding something, and that wasn't settling well with her. But he'd be at his office with Bryce and his mother all day tomorrow. That meant she'd have a car and a day. She had names and a smart head on her shoulders. She could find Donald Buchanan and Ruth Marlow. If Trevor wasn't going to give her answers, she'd get them herself.

The next morning Trevor kissed her goodbye before she'd even considered getting out of bed, but the moment the family walked out of the house she was wide awake. She climbed out of bed and went straight to her laptop and began looking for Ruth Marlow.

She jotted down the address and then called hospitals until she found the one that had Donald Buchanan as a patient. With a hand-drawn map and driving instructions, she set out to find some answers to settle her heart.

Hope wiped her hands on the sides of her jeans as she walked toward the front door of Ruth Marlow's house. Just knowing about the woman should have provided closure to her. It should have been enough to know that she was nasty to Carissa, but she couldn't help but want to see her and just be near her for even a moment.

She lifted her finger to the doorbell, but didn't push it.

Trevor had said Ruth Marlow wasn't such a bad woman. But this was Mandy Marlow's mother. Mandy Marlow, who'd abandoned her children, lied, cheated, and stole to get what she wanted.

Hope took her finger from the button and dropped her arm to her side.

This was a mistake. She was happy. David Kendal was her father and loved her very much. Sophia Kendal had sacrificed her career and everything she'd ever wanted to have her for her daughter. Carissa was her blood sister. Ruth Marlow and Donald Buchanan weren't going to change that.

She turned and started back down the steps.

"Can I help you with something?" The woman's voice came from behind her and she stopped walking. She stopped breathing.

Very slowly she turned around. Their eyes met. Shock slackened the woman's face. Hope would have known the woman just walking past her on the street. Looking at her, she would have sworn she'd known her her entire life.

Ruth raised her fingers to her lips, and tears instantly formed in her eyes. Hope stood at the base of the steps to the house and watched as Ruth Marlow stared at her.

"You're her. You're Mandy's daughter."

Hope stood paralyzed. No, she was David and Sophia's daughter. She needed to keep that in mind as much for herself as she needed Ruth Marlow to understand it too, but she couldn't speak.

Ruth started down the steps toward her. "You look just like her." She reached her hand out to touch Hope's face, but Hope flinched back. Pain flashed in Ruth's eyes. "I'm sorry," she said retracting her hand. "I just… well, seeing you… I'm sorry." She held her hand out to Hope. "I'm Ruth."

Hope shook her hand. "Hope."

"I wondered if I would get the chance to meet you. I told that man I didn't want to, but now that you're here I can't tell you how glad I am that you stopped by."

"Mrs. Marlow, I just want to know more about my birth parents. I have a very happy life. I want you to know that. But there is just that need to know."

Ruth nodded. "Did your sister come with you?"

"No."

"Well, when you do speak to her, please apologize on my behalf. Having you stand here makes me miss my daughter. The daughter I knew once." She shook her head and crossed her arms over her chest. "I wasn't very nice to your sister when she called years and years ago. I suppose I should have been nicer."

"She understands."

"Please, will you come in?"

"Thank you."

As she followed Ruth back into her house, a wall of unexpected emotion. Hope sucked it back. She wasn't going to cry or get attached. This was a journey she'd almost walked away from. A few moments with the woman wasn't going to hurt. She would be gracious and then leave. Suddenly she was missing Kansas City terribly.

"I have some iced tea," Ruth offered.

"That would be wonderful." Hope followed her through the well-decorated home to the kitchen, where her refrigerator was covered in old school pictures of Mandy that resembled her own. There were drawings in crayon, signed by Mandy, and more pictures of her with a boy a few years older. A grocery list hung with the old mementos, reminding Hope that Ruth lived day to day among her memories. How could Mandy, the woman Hope knew to hop beds, do drugs, and live in run-down motels have grown up in such a normal place? "You have a lovely home."

"Mandy never thought so." Ruth pursed her lips and let out a slow breath. "I'm sorry. I should just let you ask questions and keep opinions and comments to myself." She handed Hope a glass and gestured to the table for her to sit.

"I don't know what to ask. I mean I've had a million questions and now suddenly I've drawn a blank."

Ruth sat down across from Hope and wrapped her hands around the tall glass of tea she'd poured for herself. "Well, let me tell you that Mandy wasn't always the person you probably know her to be. The little girl I raised loved to paint. She loved to dance and swim. She was a good student." Ruth shook her head. "She had a brother she was very close to. He was only two years older than she was. The world—her world—revolved around him." Her brows knit and she chewed on her lip before taking a sip of her tea. "He was killed when she was fourteen. From the moment we told her he was gone, she snapped, she changed."

"I'm sorry for your loss. I didn't know." She couldn't imagine if she'd lost Carissa. Her life revolved around her sister. What would that have done to her? Obviously it was a life-changing event for Mandy.

"It was such a long time ago. I thought it was a phase. The drugs, the shoplifting, the older men." She sipped her drink again, and her hand shook. "I lost my son, and then a few years later my daughter's grief took her from me too."

Ruth stood and dumped her tea into the sink and set her glass on the counter. "Tell me about you," she said, her hands gripping the edge of the counter. "Tell me who you are."

"Well." Hope collected her thoughts. First and foremost, sitting in the very home that Mandy grew up in, she realized she was most proud to be David and Sophia Kendal's daughter. "I'm an artist. I paint, using all mediums. I like photography too." She stood and held tight to the back of her chair. "I own a small store and sell my art and small gifts. I can't play an instrument, but my sister— now, she's an amazing musician." She smiled, thinking of her sister. Carissa had helped to shape her into the very person she was. "My parents made sure I was a Girl Scout, that I played sports, and I went to church almost every Sunday. My sister made sure I understood how much they all wanted and loved me, and she's always taken extra special care of me."

Pride was swelling in her heart and in her voice. She was just getting started. "My mother is a cellist. My father a retired pilot. I have two nephews and two nieces who are my life." Why she needed to be in Ruth's kitchen to understand the perfect life she had, she wasn't sure.

Ruth turned toward her. "You sound happy."

"I was. I mean I am." Hope reached for her purse next to her chair. "I should go."

"Hope, I'm glad Mandy gave you to your family. She couldn't have given you a life like you had. It makes me happy to know my granddaughters were taken care of. Your father is an amazing man."

"Thank you."

"Thank you for stopping by and meeting me. I feel like I might have closure now."

Hope watched Ruth's face soften. She needed to walk out of the house and keep walking. She needed to say goodbye to Ruth Marlow and leave it at that.

But she didn't. "Would you like to meet Carissa and her children? Your great-grandchildren."

Ruth's lips tightened as she warded off tears Hope could see already welling in her eyes.

"I'm sure you don't need me in your life. Your sister has been long removed from Mandy's neglect."

"You're not Mandy's neglect. You obviously were a victim of her neglect too. I am your granddaughter. You should have had the pleasure of having your family back. I'm offering that to you. If you want it, that is."

Ruth brushed her tears away from her cheeks. "It's been a very long time since I had any family. I would love to get to know you and your sister."

Hope smiled as part of that hole she'd needed to mend began to heal. Mandy had hurt too many people, and now they could heal each other.

Having not walked away from Ruth Marlow, Hope drove to the hospital, realizing she had to meet Donald Buchanan. She'd come that far, and she had to follow through.

Her knees shook as she stepped off the floor to the ICU. She waited by the desk for someone to guide her to the right area.

A nurse with a sweet smile and a blonde ponytail that swung when she walked spotted her first.

"Can I help you?"

"I'm looking for Donald Buchanan."

The nurse tightened her lips. "Only family. I'm sorry."

Hope nodded and sucked in a deep breath. "I'm his daughter." The words were out, but they felt foul.

"Oh." The nurse's eyes widened and she smiled. "I met your brothers last week. Handsome."

A lump formed in her throat. Hope swallowed it and managed a smile. Brothers. That was a lot to take in.

"He's right back here if you want to follow me." Hope fell in next to the nurse. "His wife hasn't been in to see him all week. Your brothers said she's a nasty thing. I understand that. I have a stepmother too." Then as though she'd said something wrong, the nurse snapped her head toward Hope with horror in her eyes. "Oh, dear. His wife isn't your mother, is she?"

"No."

"Thank goodness. I have a tendency to talk too much." She pushed back a curtain. "Here you go. He's in and out of consciousness. So he might not be too responsive."

"Thank you," Hope said, trying to keep her voice even so the woman wouldn't know this was the first time she'd laid eyes on the man.

"You holler if you need anything."

"I will."

The nurse slid out of the small room and Hope stood at the door and stared. He was old. Old and very frail. His hair was snow white and his skin pale, almost transparent. Monitors to his side kept his stats and a tube of oxygen in his nose gave him breath.

This was not her father, and upon looking at him, she felt that surge through her like a spike of electricity. She needed to turn away, call David, and apologize for making the journey.

"Mandy." The sound was weak and airy, but she realized it came from the frail man in the bed. "Mandy."

Hope's lips trembled, and her heart rate kicked up when she noticed the man was staring up at her. She willed her feet to move her closer, and his shaking hand reached for her.

"Mandy, you came back." He even managed a smile and it broke Hope's heart. She took his outreached hand in her own.

"My name is Hope."

"Hope." A tear slid from his eye and a sliver of a smile crossed his dry, cracked lips. "Our daughter."

That shook Hope down to her core. He knew who she was.

"You know me?"

He gave the very slightest nod.

"I thought you didn't know who I was." Now the tears threatened her eyes. "I thought she hid me from you."

"She did," he said weakly. "That man found you for me."

"That man? You had someone find me?"

He closed his eyes. When he opened them, Hope was sure she saw clarity in them. It was almost as if her holding his hand was giving him strength.

"I only found out about you." He was quiet a moment as he drew in an extra breath, then continued. "I couldn't let my wife find out."

"Why?" She wiped at the tears that now fell freely.

"I gave Mandy what was hers." He paused again. "She deserved what her father had left her."

"The stocks?"

He only nodded.

"She didn't tell you she had your child?"

He shook his head and there was a sadness that filled his drawn face. "I was married. But I was in love with Mandy."

In all her life, she'd never heard someone speak as fondly of Mandy as Donald Buchanan did.

"So you found me?" Hope sniffed back tears, trying to compose herself.

Donald nodded weakly again. "Jacobs."

Hope's mouth dropped open and her racing heart plunged into her stomach. "You sent Trevor Jacobs to find me?"

He nodded.

"You paid him to find me for you?"

"It wasn't cheap, but it was worth it." He smiled up at her and she tried to keep her calm, but it was fading fast. She'd never felt so betrayed in all of her life. Her knees wobbled beneath her and her free hand clenched at her side.

She had been sure that the journey to New York was going to prove that Mandy Marlow was a liar, a thief, and a cheat, and then she'd be able to put the woman behind her and move on with her life. She never would have guessed the man she'd given her heart too fit the bill as well.

Hope felt sick.

The curtain opened and the nurse stepped in. "Ma'am, I'm afraid you'll have to go. Visitors can only stay for a few minutes."

Hope looked down at her biological father. His eyes were filled with love. Did he see her or Mandy?

"Come back again," he said softly.

She couldn't say anything. She bent down, kissed his cold cheek, and left him, unsure whether she'd ever see him again.

Chapter Twelve

The churning in Hope's stomach only worsened when she heard Trevor's voice.

"Hope! Hope, where are you?"

Violet's voice was softer. "She's packing."

"She's what?" He burst through the bedroom door. "There you are."

There was an enormous grin on his face and he waved a sheaf of papers at her. It was as if he didn't understand the implications of what she was doing.

"Your father is a genius. A dammed genius."

"Not news to me, pal." She moved past him and tucked clothes into the suitcase, which lay open on the bed.

"He caught Delores Buchanan."

Those words stopped her. She turned, and he held up the papers in his hand.

"She's been arrested and so has her merry band of thieves." He pulled her to him. "Your father, sister, and Thomas pulled her in, and she fell into their trap. Genius!"

"What are you talking about?" She deliberately took a step away from him.

"They set her up. They knew she'd go after Carissa next. She knew you'd been to the bank and had the stocks. So Thomas and Carissa set up their house to be hit, and sure enough she had one of her people hit it. He was arrested while in the house and in order to lessen the charges he spilled. Oh, how spilled." He laughed. "I think your dad said he sang like a canary."

"Too many movies."

"Either way. She went to your shop looking for you like they thought she would, and that's where they took her down. She's out of your life and out of the way."

"Fine." She turned back to the suitcase and threw in another blouse.

"What are you doing?"

"Leaving."

"What?" He grabbed her hand as she picked up another shirt. "Why? What's going on?"

"Why don't you tell me, you lying snake?"

Trevor stood before her, his eyes wide, his expression hurt.

"Oh, you're good aren't you? You play all the parts so well." She pulled her hand from his grasp and threw in another blouse before turning toward him and dropping her hands in anger. "I met Donald Buchanan today."

Trevor tipped his head back as if she'd slapped him in the face.

Hope pursed her lips. That was all she needed. "He paid you to find me. So you did. Wormed your way right into my heart and into my bed. What an idiot I am."

"Hope." He touched her shoulder, but she shook off his hand.

"You made me think I was hiring you to find him, but all along I was the prize. He sent you to find me." She stopped and wiped at her eyes. He wasn't worth the tears. "You lied to me from the minute I met you."

"It's not like that, Hope."

"Liar!" She slammed closed the suitcase and zipped it up. "Did you know I have two brothers? Did you know that?"

"Well…" He rubbed the back of his neck. "Did you talk to the blonde nurse?"

"Ye-e-e-es," she said.

"Yeah, that would have been me and Bryce. Don't worry." He held up his hands. "We are not your brothers. We just needed to gain access to Buchanan."

Hope shook her head. "You're in so deep you can't even tell the truth."

She pulled the suitcase from the bed and it thudded to the floor. Fighting with the handle, she managed to pull it up and roll the case it to the door, but Trevor was faster.

"Listen, I deserve a moment to have you hear me out."

"You don't deserve shit." She tried for the door, but he blocked her.

"Don't walk out on me. I love you."

"It doesn't work anymore, Mr. Jacobs. You can't lie your way into my heart and expect me to pool at your feet. I might be young and I might have been naive, but I'm not anymore. Get out of my way."

Trevor moved closer to her with his head hung low. "Stay. Please Stay."

There was a tapping on the door. "Hope's taxi is here," Violet softly said from the other side.

Hope reached for the door, and Trevor gently touched her hand. "He did hire me."

It was enough truth to make Hope release the door, but she wouldn't lift her eyes to look into his. She'd give him two minutes, but it wasn't going to change anything.

Trevor shoved the paper he carried into his back pocket. "I was hired by Donald Buchanan to find Mandy Marlow. I did that. I found her in a cemetery in Kansas City. He was looking for her because he came into the knowledge that he had a daughter. You, Hope."

She kept her eyes focused on the back of the door, but he continued.

"When you were born, Ruth got a letter from your great-grandmother Katie, telling her that Mandy had died and there was a baby. She thought it was a scam for money so she didn't think much about it. Recently Delores Buchanan must have found out that Mandy died and she was looking for the payoff money she'd given her to disappear with the baby. Buchanan found out about you, but Delores has always known."

"So what's the payoff, Trevor? Do you get a cut? I'm worth what to you?"

"Hope, what happened between us is real. Yes, I was sent to find you and get to know you."

Her head snapped up. He was making it worse than she could have imagined. "Get to know me. Well you certainly did, didn't you?"

"Stay. Let me keep you safe until I know everything is behind us."

"Right. Stay with the man who stalked me. Get out of my way, Trevor."

She pushed past him and opened the door. Violet stood just a few feet away.

"Thank you for letting me stay, Mrs. Jacobs." She walked past her and out the front door. The driver threw her suitcase into the trunk and she looked back only once to see Violet holding her son by the arm on the front porch.

Hope sank into the seat. She loved him and that hurt most of all. He lied to her and now she had to move on without him.

Trevor hit brick walls when he tried to contact Hope the week after she'd fled. Damn caller ID. She wouldn't answer his calls at her shop. When he had Bryce call from his cell phone, she hung up on him as soon as she realized who he was.

There was no luck reaching her through Carissa or Thomas, and he absolutely feared talking to David. Sophia had had kind words, though she wouldn't let him talk to Hope.

Violet set the mail on the counter and rested a large package against the cupboard as she walked in the kitchen. Her high heel shoes clicked on the tile floor.

"I figured I'd find you here," she said, leaning against the counter and scanning a look over her son. "Have you sat here all day with your cell phone in your hand?"

"I've tried six times to get her to talk to me. I left six messages and she refuses to talk to me." He dropped the phone and rested his elbows on the table. He tangled his fingers into his hair and held his head. "It's been a week."

"You were an ass."

"Thanks, Mom."

"Really, how did you think this was going to end?"

"I didn't expect to fall in love with her."

Violet let out a sigh, walked to her son, and ran her hand over his hair, forcing him to drop his hands. "That's when it always happens."

She walked back to the package she'd set on the floor. "This came for you today." She picked it up and looked at it. "It's from Kansas City. That's a positive sign, isn't it?"

"No." He huffed out a breath as he stood up and took it from her. "Sit down."

Violet released her hold and sat down at the table.

"This was supposed to be for your birthday."

"My birthday isn't for a few weeks."

"Exactly. We'd planned to bring it with us, but we decided to ship it."

"We?" Violet raised her eyebrows.

"Hope and I." He handed her the package and she held it upright on her lap. "I wanted this to be so much more.

She should be here." He waited for her to open it so he could see her expression.

"Oh, Trevor." Her shoulders dropped, her eyes went soft, and her fingers pressed against her trembling lips.

She was touched, just as he knew she would be.

"You like it?"

"Love it. Love it!" She wiped a tear that rolled down her cheek. "Hope did this?"

"Yes."

"I'm a good mother, you know. I did my homework and looked into her. Her record is clean."

He let out a weak laugh. "I know."

"But she does some very nice work. This, however…" She studied the painting closer. "This is beyond anything she shows on her website."

"She painted it after I met her. From memory." He sat down in the chair across the table. "When I walked through her shop the first time, it was there. It was only a drawing, but it was me."

"She's captured your very spirit in this painting. The light in your eyes, the subtle pout of your lips. She's in love with you." Her eyes shifted to his and calmed him just as his mother could always do.

"She might have been."

"Still is. That's why she won't talk to you. You're too embedded in her heart."

"I miss her."

"Things will come around. If it's meant to be, it will all work out."

He nodded, hoping she was right, and really, when wasn't she? But it hurt. He'd never had pain that squeezed his heart and threatened to choke him like the pain of losing Hope did.

Bryce had managed to put the office back together after the break in. And with them both assuming Trevor wasn't returning, he'd taken the bigger desk.

Trevor didn't mind. Bryce's desk looked out over the busy streets of New York, and it took his mind off the serenity of Kansas City.

He'd followed up on a few cases he'd left unfinished, but Bryce had been fairly efficient while he'd been gone.

He made a few phone calls to find out the status of Delores Buchanan's arrest and holding. She wouldn't be bothering Hope or her family ever again.

A smile crept across his lips. David and Thomas had never struck him as the PI type, but they just might come in handy someday. Well, that would be if he were to have cases in Kansas City again.

He tipped back in his chair and kicked his feet up on the desk. The lunch crowds were making their way into the streets and the hot dog cart on the corner already had a line.

"Hey." Bryce broke the silence of the office. He stood in the doorway, both hands braced on the jambs. A look of worry curtained his expression.

Trevor dropped his feet and stood. "What's up? You look spooked."

Bryce sucked in a breath as he took a step inside the office. He dropped his shoulders, bit his lip, and shifted his eyes back to Trevor. "I thought you should know. Donald Buchanan passed away last night."

Trevor felt his legs give out and he sat in the chair beneath him. He felt his throat closing up with tears. They weren't for the man who had passed, but for the girl who had only just met him.

Bryce set a folded piece of paper on the desk. "His service is on Friday."

"I'll be there." He picked up the announcement and read it over.

"Hey, pal, I'm really sorry it worked out this way. I've got your back. Whatever you need."

"Thanks. I'll be okay." The words were out, but they didn't ring true in his heart.

His mother offered to go to the funeral with him; even his father had offered, hesitantly. But he thought it best to go alone. He was hopeful that Hope would be there. Though he didn't expect her to be alone, he wanted a moment to talk to her.

When he walked across the grass to the plot where Donald Buchanan would be laid to rest, he felt a pang of sadness. There was only a small gathering of people, and no one sat in the family seats.

The service went quickly and Trevor kept his eyes roaming, looking for Hope to arrive, but she didn't.

Once the service was over a gentle gloved hand touched his arm. He turned to see Ruth Marlow, her eyes shielded by large, round sunglasses, standing beside him.

She was dressed in black and had even donned a black hat. He hadn't seen her among the crowd. Then again he hadn't been looking for her.

"Mrs. Marlow, it's nice to see you."

"You too, Mr. Jacobs." She patted his arm. "I was sorry to hear that he passed." She looked at the grave. "He'd have liked to have the chance to get to know her better."

"I thought she'd be here."

Ruth nodded. "She was with him when he died."

He staggered backward. She'd been in New York and hadn't called or dropped by. She'd avoided him. He swiped the back of his hand over his brow. The heat was getting to him. "Hope was here? In New York?"

"She came in with her mother and father." Ruth shifted. "It's hot. Why don't we sit?"

Trevor agreed and moved toward the chairs. "Did you see her while she was here?"

Ruth sat straighter and held tight to her little shiny black purse. "Yes. She called to let me know they were coming. The hospital had contacted her when he'd started to fail. They flew right out."

"I would have thought she'd call me."

"She's upset. You understand."

He nodded and he despised himself for it. "You met her parents, then?"

Ruth smiled brightly. "Yes. They came to the house and we had dinner. David was as nice as I remembered, and Sophia, well, she's just a genuinely wonderful woman. My Mandy did well when she gave Hope to them. They love her so much."

"You didn't meet Carissa?"

"No. But I'll be there for Thanksgiving. Sophia invited me herself."

At least Donald Buchanan's search for his daughter had netted Ruth Marlow some peace. She had a family again.

Ruth took a handkerchief from her purse and dabbed her eyes under her large glasses. "She brought me a painting."

Trevor lifted his head. "Did she?"

"A beautiful sunset. Just like the one my Mandy painted." She let out a sigh and took a deep breath. Then she took her hand and laid it on Trevor's. "She misses you."

He felt the quiver of hope run through him and it threatened to turn to tears, but he wasn't going to shed them.

Ruth replaced the handkerchief into her purse. "Give her some time. She has a lot going on in that beautiful head of hers right now. But my granddaughter is a smart one. She'll do what's right. Besides"—she stood next to him and looked down—"Donald liked you. He'd be happy to know you were together again."

She said her goodbye, and the small crowd that had lingered at the grave dispersed. Trevor sat alone, the casket of Donald Buchanan still only a few feet away.

"I promise, if she forgives me, I will forever take care of her."

A breeze blew through the tent and the scent of lilacs carried on it. Trevor closed his eyes and breathed it in. It was familiar, but not for any reason he could think of.

He decided it was time to go and put his life back together. With or without Hope. He pushed to his feet and walked to the casket. On the ground two white daises lay with their yellow centers staring up at him. Trevor bent down and picked them up. He looked for matching flowers in an arrangement, but there weren't any. Only the two he had found on the ground.

He reached to lay them on Donald's casket and as he did, he felt the shock of electricity race through his fingers, just like the day he'd met Hope. He pulled back his hand and gave it a shake. And then he smiled.

"It's a sign, Hope. Daisies. All women in your family like daisies." He gave a laugh. "I'll bet that would include your great-grandmother and your great-aunt as well."

There was a bubble of excitement that nearly burst within him. He'd been chosen. Donald Buchanan had chosen him for his little girl, whether he had meant to or not, and the universe was telling him not to give up.

No, he wouldn't give up. He loved Hope, and by God he was going to marry her.

From his office in New York, Trevor managed to find himself an apartment in Kansas City. He gave some thought to the distance from Hope's shop and her home and made sure it was far enough he couldn't be accused of stalking her. He'd only signed a six-month lease; when things worked out, they'd need a bigger place.

He'd organized his client folders and made notes. He'd hand them over to Bryce without another thought. He deserved them for having put up with Trevor for so long.

The tap at the door was welcome when he saw his mother standing in the doorway in her pristine blue suit.

"I just received this in the office." She held up a file folder. "It's one of my clients, but the request was made for you to deliver it."

Trevor pushed back in his chair and gave chuckle. "What are you talking about?"

"It seems that Carmichael Industries purchased the medical supply company last year."

"You picked up that account." He rose from his chair and walked toward her. "You wined, dined, and impressed the socks off of Peter Carmichael with your backswing on the tennis court."

She smiled broadly. "I sure did."

"Okay, what does this have to do with me?"

"Well, this medical supply was formerly owned by Donald Buchanan."

Trevor shook his head. What a tidy package.

Violet stepped into the office further. "He gave this to Peter Carmichael during the merger. He told Peter that upon his death there were specific instructions on what he was to do with it."

"And he was supposed to give it to me?"

"Yes." She handed him the file.

Trevor opened it and dumped its contents on his desk. In the envelope were stock certificates, just like the ones Hope and Carissa had found in Mandy's safe-deposit box. With them was a letter that stated upon Buchanan's death the stocks that were still in his name were to go to Mandy Marlow and one Trevor Jacobs was to deliver them to her. Or, since she had died, to her children.

Trevor handed the letter back to his mother. "This must have been about the time he learned there was a daughter. He had every intention of using me to find Mandy and Hope."

"Looks like it."

"But why would he still have stocks?"

"Carmichael would have used that in the deal. Lots of mergers happen that way. They give the prior owner stock options."

"Carmichael doesn't know about the other stocks, then."

"What stocks?"

"The ones Donald Buchanan gave to Mandy after her father died."

Violet smiled widely. "Well, it looks like your girlfriend and her sister just became very wealthy."

He nodded and then swallowed the lump in his throat. "I have to deliver these to her."

"Yes, you do."

"She has to see me now. I guess I can give them all to Carissa, but…" A smile as wide as his mother's settled on his face. "I love you, Mom."

"I know you do, Son. I'll miss you now that you'll be living in Kansas City. But you'll visit often, right?"

"You can bet on it."

It was a Saturday and Hope was grateful. It had been a rough few weeks, but Saturdays were busy and that kept her mind off Trevor and the loss of Donald Buchanan.

She rang up a sale and had four other guests shopping for gifts.

As she finished the sale and the guest walked out the door, she looked back to see four sets of eyes peering through the glass and she smiled. Her nieces and nephews were the one thing that would forever make her happy.

Hope walked around the corner of the counter, and they all marched in like little soldiers in a row. They had their hands tucked behind their backs and very serious looks on their faces.

"My goodness, what are the four of you up to?"

"These are for you," Becky said as she handed her three daisies.

"Daisies are my favorite."

"I know." Becky smiled.

The other three followed suit as the door opened and Trevor walked in with a bouquet of daisies in one hand and a large envelope in the other. He stood at the door, the kids at his side and now the peering eyes of her sister had arrived in the window.

Hope stiffened, though inside she was all sorts of mush for the sentiment.

"Trevor. What are you doing here?"

"I'm groveling. I'm begging. I'm pleading. I'm—"

"I get it."

He stepped to her and handed her the flowers. "I'm an"—he looked at the little people standing behind him—"a butt. A big, fat, sorry butt."

The children giggled.

Hope bit the inside of her cheek so as not to laugh. "You are a butt."

"I know. My mother didn't raise me to be one, but all the same I became one and I'm sorry."

"Apology accepted." She finally smiled. "But what do you want? I'm busy."

He handed her the large gold envelope, and she exchanged glances with him.

"What is this?"

"Your biological father left that for you. Well, for you and Carissa. Okay, he left it for Mandy."

"You're babbling."

He wiped his hands on his pants and then shoved them into his pockets. "I'm nervous."

"Why?"

"Because I love you and I'm afraid you don't love me anymore."

She took a breath to steady herself. He loved her. Well, she could see that in his eyes, no matter what he'd done before. But for the moment she liked that he was nervous around her.

Hope walked back to the counter, slid out the contents of the envelope, and looked up at him. No matter how badly she'd tried to let her feelings go, she couldn't. "My biggest problem is that I still love you and don't know how to get over it."

She looked down at the pile she'd slid from the envelope and tried to make sense of it. She read the letter, focused in on the part where Donald knew Trevor would know where to find her, and shook her head.

"He left us his stocks? Well, he left them to Mandy?"

"Yes."

"So we own these and the ones Mandy left us?"

"Yes."

Her eyes widened and she let out an unsteady breath. "Wow. I don't know what else to say."

"Well that's all I guess I had to do." He turned to walk to the door. Four sets of eyes still lingered on him.

"Trevor, you know that my family is really big into matchmaking." She walked around the side of the counter as he turned around.

"You've mentioned it."

"Well, without Grandma Katie and Aunt Millie, I figured I'd never have my chance. But it looks like my biological father was a matchmaker of sorts."

"I suppose it does." He walked toward her.

"So, given the fact that in my dreams Grandma told you'd come, and Donald actually sent you for me—twice— I guess I have to look at that as a sign."

"Do you believe in signs, Hope?"

"I think I do."

She was right in front of him now, and there was that electricity buzzing between them again. He felt it too. She saw it in his eyes.

Trevor reached into his pocket and pulled out a small black box. Her breath hitched and she met his eyes as he opened it.

She let out a little gasp and he smiled. "Would you consider this a sign?" He took the princess-cut diamond ring from the box and held it out to her.

Hope raised her fingers to her mouth. "Trevor, do you think this is really wise?"

"Matchmakers and signs. I don't see any way around it."

The guests who had been shopping were now gathered around, and Carissa had stepped into the shop.

Trevor got down on one knee and took her hand. "I've made some huge mistakes and I'm sorry for them. But they led me to you, and I fell in love with you the moment I saw your face in a picture. Hope, I want you to be my wife. I want to have children with you and I want you to paint their faces on canvas just as you did mine."

"Trevor." She gulped in air, trying to keep the happy sob that bubbled in her throat from escaping.

"I want to wake with you every morning for the rest of my life, and I want to grow very old with you and have Sunday dinners at our house."

"I can't do that." She looked at him, keeping her face straight.

"Oh." His face drained of color and the smile disappeared from his lips.

"Sunday dinner belongs at my mom's house. We can do Saturday."

The color returned to his cheeks and a smile to his lips. He shook his head and let out a loud breath. "You'll marry me?"

"I'll marry you."

He slid the ring on her finger and stood back up. Hope wrapped her arms around his neck, and he wrapped his around her waist.

"I'll make you happy, Hope."

"You'd better." But she knew he would. She'd know it since she saw him in her dreams.

Epilogue

Hope wore Aunt Millie's dress and her Grandma Katie's veil. The necklace her grandmother had given her mother, who had passed it to Carissa, who had then given to her, hung prominently on her neck. In Donald Buchanan's belongings, which she'd been given, were a pair of cufflinks with embedded diamonds, which Trevor wore on his shirt, and they caught the sunlight as her father walked her down the aisle toward him.

Hope carried a bouquet of daisies, and so did her sister and her nieces.

It was her turn to marry in the backyard of her sister's house. Her grandmother had married there as well as her grandparents, parents, and her sister. Spring surrounded them and embraced them with the blooming of flowers and the fresh green leaves on the trees.

David hugged her tightly as he stopped before Trevor. She smiled up at him, and a tear lingered in his eye. She kissed him softly on the cheek. She loved him so much and was so grateful for everything that had led her to him.

David turned to Trevor, shook his hand, and then pulled him into a hug.

"Take care of her."

"I promise, sir."

David took his seat next to his wife, and Hope watched as Ruth pulled a handkerchief from her purse and handed it Violet, who then dabbed her eyes with it.

Trevor said he'd take her as his wife and she responded in kind. The minister led them into prayers of thanks, and Hope realized she'd never been more thankful than she was at that moment.

And as Hope kissed her husband, the wind blew through the yard. The scent of lilacs floated in the air, and two daisies fell at her feet. Trevor smiled as he picked them up and tucked them into her hair.

"A match made in heaven."

Hope lifted her eyes to the sky where the sun filtered through the clouds and rays of shimmery light cast down on her as if her grandmother and aunt were embracing her with the warmth. She looked at her husband and lifted her hand to his cheek. "And what a heavenly match it is."

Meet the author

Damon Kappel ©2009

Bestselling Author Bernadette Marie is known for building families readers want to be part of. Her series *The Keller Family* has graced bestseller charts since its release in 2011, along with her other series and single title books. The married mother of five sons promises *Happily Ever After always*...and says she can write it, because she lives it.

When not writing, Bernadette Marie is shuffling her sons to their many events—mostly hockey—and enjoying the beautiful views of the Colorado Rocky Mountains from her front step. She is also an accomplished martial artist with a second degree black belt in Tang Soo Do.

A chronic entrepreneur, Bernadette Marie opened her own publishing house in 2011, *5 Prince Publishing*, so that she could publish the books she liked to write and help make the dreams of other aspiring authors come true too.

www.bernadettemarie.com
www.5princebooks.com/bernadettemarie.html
www.facebook.com/authorbernadettemarie.com
@writesromance on Twitter
info@bernadettmarie.com

www.ingramcontent.com/pod-product-compliance
Lightning Source LLC
Chambersburg PA
CBHW030408020726
47493CB00003B/979